The SMElting Cauldron

Raj Raman holds an engineering degree from NIT Rourkela and a postgraduate degree in Management (PGDM) from IIM Bangalore. He has a rich and diverse experience of over thirty years across industries from manufacturing to services, and has been instrumental in the growth and establishment of a number of these enterprises. His stints across the country have enabled him to appreciate and deal with the nuances of a diverse country like India.

He has led a number of organizations, and also served on their boards. He currently owns and runs a successful boutique consulting firm, specializing in SMEs, supporting and enabling their growth and expansion, while playing the role of a coach and mentor to the promoters and entrepreneurs at the helm of such companies.

The SMElting Cauldron
STEELING THE BACKBONE OF THE ECONOMY

Raj Raman

RUPA

Published by
Rupa Publications India Pvt. Ltd 2018
7/16, Ansari Road, Daryaganj
New Delhi 110002

Sales centres:
Allahabad Bengaluru Chennai
Hyderabad Jaipur Kathmandu
Kolkata Mumbai

Copyright © Raj Raman 2018

All rights reserved.
No part of this publication may be reproduced, transmitted, or stored in a retrieval system, in any form or by any means, electronic, mechanical, photocopying, recording or otherwise, without the prior permission of the publisher.

This is a work of fiction based on the experiences, views and opinions of the author. Names, organizations, places and incidents are either the product of the author's imagination or are used fictitiously and any resemblance to any actual person, living or dead, organization, event or locale is entirely coincidental.

ISBN: 978-93-5304-131-1

First Impression 2018

10 9 8 7 6 5 4 3 2 1

The moral right of the author has been asserted.

Printed at Parksons Graphics Pvt. Ltd, Mumbai.

This book is sold subject to the condition that it shall not, by way of trade or otherwise, be lent, resold, hired out, or otherwise circulated, without the publisher's prior consent, in any form of binding or cover other than that in which it is published.

This book is dedicated to the Indian entrepreneurs of small and medium enterprises, the true backbone of the Indian economy. It is a testimony to their commitment, passion, drive and dedication, which enable them to negotiate the treacherous, confusing, challenging and at times frustrating nuances of the environment that is India. Their desire, intent, passion, ambition and drive, help create a sustainable enterprise; a yeoman exercise, to say the least in the evolving economy of India, which is a mosaic of paradoxes.

Contents

Foreword by Harsh C. Mariwala — xi

Introduction — xiii

The Hiring Dilemma: The paradoxes that the promoter faces, as one attempts to transit from self-driven to professional day-to-day running of the enterprise. Are there any easy answers? — 1

The Ca(sh)tch 22 Situation: Uncertainties and challenges of growth and profitability, and the tightrope walk; trade-offs involved and the cashflow conundrum. Funding growth, can he cash in? — 6

Capital Crimes: The attraction of private equity investment, but are they all they are touted to be? Hidden agendas, personal priorities and undercurrents of Machiavellian manipulations, can make it a path of landmines. — 14

Taxing Times: Entrepreneurs and the challenges of managing stated profitability; do we pay a substantial tax to the government, or do we succumb to ways and means to camouflage the profits? The risks and pitfalls. — 23

Debts And Don'ts: Borrowing to fund growth seems simple and logical. However, there are hidden costs, processes and compliances, which one tends to ignore. Total cost of debt and size are both key! — 29

Growth Pangs: Growth through acquisitions is fraught with challenges; synergies, market dynamics, disclosures, people strengths, culture and experience, all play a major role. Do venture with your eyes open! — 36

Greed Expectations: The temptation of scale, aided by the booming sector made real estate an easy hunting ground in the late 2000s; the nexuses, the superlative returns and the prevailing business practices, test values and morals! — 43

Changing Paradigms And Strategic Shifts: A B2C business comes with its set of challenges, especially one with a product and distribution angle, and an aspirational positioning. Most promoters do not think it through. — 50

Reality Aftershocks: Early successes, and capital aplenty, tend to lead ventures up the path of celebrating early; a few rough years, mounting cost structures, poor economic evaluations, create downward spirals. — 59

No Free Lunches: Entrepreneurs often get confronted with deals and opportunities that are too good to be true, and they often are! Shortcuts to success are fraught with unknowns which extract their price! — 66

The Perils Of Legacy: Acquiring a small and medium enterprise means legacy costs, manpower, processes and practices. It requires a very strong eye for detail, to ensure these do not become a weight around the neck. ... 74

Bootstrapping To a Fault: The challenge of a startup, the tussles and struggles which promoters go through, and the risk of giving up too early, or not committing to it fully, is the dilemma of most of them. ... 81

Justifying Means To What End: The challenge that an entrepreneur faces when confronted with a downward economy, a few tough months, poor cash flows, no succour drives him to desert prudence. ... 89

Controlled Risks And Managed Growth: In a high growth market, it is critical to manage growth and not get taken in by large opportunities. Ability to digest adversity and losses is key! ... 96

Scaling Highs And Lows: Scaling a business which is driven by cash earnings, has its own set of sacrosanct principles. Any attempt to short circuit presents a cascading disaster waiting to happen. ... 104

The Valuation Trap: Valuations range from the ridiculous to the absurd in turbulent times, especially in the technology and e-commerce space. Accepting this fact, makes it easier to raise capital, or exit a business. ... 115

Technology Selling Paradoxes: Selling cutting-edge technology products is a challenge for most entrepreneurs. The process of creating a market for the same is distinct from the usual business development approaches. ... 122

The Need To Call It Quits: The constantly evolving   129
environment sometimes makes apparently successful
business models, redundant. Constant recalibration can
save serious heartburn.

Afterword   137

Acknowledgements   141

Foreword

Small and medium enterprises are truly the backbone of the Indian economy. These fifty million or so organizations, spread over the length and breadth of the country, are a tribute to the entrepreneurship of the promoters. Against all odds, they have created and sustained businesses, that are the fabric of a throbbing and thriving S&MEs segment of industry.

Having worked closely with these entrepreneurs through our Foundation, Ascent, I have had the privilege to closely observe and interact with these passionate individuals, who have managed to create and build successful business enterprises. Their trials and tribulations are sometimes extreme and heart-wrenching, and they do need support, encouragement and motivation, in all forms and manner possible.

This book resonates with all that I have seen and observed. It has captured the diverse set of challenges and the subtle nuances of the environment that these entrepreneurs have to deal with on a regular basis. Each story very realistically captures these moments in the journey of every enterprise. It provides a pragmatic and realistic view of the organizations and the minds of the promoters, and all the turmoil they see.

The stories have been presented in readable and easy-to-comprehend format, making it simple to understand and appreciate. The problems and challenges in each, are all very practical and real issues that SMEs contend with, and the possible resolutions mentioned, are all common sense and doable.

This book is a good read for all those who would like to either be an entrepreneur, or who would like to be part of the ecosystem that supports and boosts the S&MEs and the entrepreneurs who lead them. It is also a good surrogate, close-up view for budding investors, bankers, regulators and keen students of this segment.

Harsh C. Mariwala
Chairman, Marico Limited
May 2018

Introduction

It is an established fact that small and medium enterprises (S&MEs) constitute the backbone of Indian economy. Contributing to over 80 per cent of employment generation, 45 per cent of exports and 37 per cent of the GDP, these small microcosms of industry, survive and grow amidst a plethora of challenges brought about by the environment, be it political, regulatory, social or geographic. An entrepreneur has to deal with all of these to the best of his ability, and emerge from this SMElting cauldron, a smarter, wiser, businessperson taking his organization to the next level of growth, profitability and success.

Entrepreneurs come in many hues, shapes and sizes, and hail from diverse regions, castes, creeds and religions which add to their uniqueness. But their underlying sense of purpose, relentless drive and ambition, and optimism, even under grave circumstances, make them a unique breed. Across sectors, industries and social strata, we see them going about their tasks, under varying and challenging circumstances, environments, dealing with the vagaries of the support system.

Having worked closely with the S&MEs of various forms and across sectors and geographies, I have learnt to admire their grit and determination, which is a special requirement in the Indian environment. They have demonstrated repeatedly that trying circumstances only strengthen their resolve to confront, circumnavigate, engage, beat and surmount the challenges posed by the political, social, regulatory and financial systems that exist in India. It never ceases to amaze me, how simple processes can become deal breakers of a business created over decades of labour, effort and application.

The unique experiences that each one of them encounters are learnings for generations to come. The fabric of the value system of each entrepreneur shapes the routes and methods that he adopts for success, which is their primary driver. I have attempted to present here, some of those experiences, circumstances, behaviours and challenges that emerge, and can be observed when we deal with the SME segment, and its unique band of players. They probably face the toughest tests in the early stages, and it is rightly said that the first million is the most difficult to make.

The stories that follow are all based on fictitious characters and companies. They are a figment of my imagination, and should be viewed as my attempts at being creative. However, they are based on my personal experiences with SMEs across the country. The incidences are drawn from that rich repertoire of cases I have dealt with over a few decades. They represent a sample of what are the realities of building a business in India, with its varied nuances of social behaviour, cultural heritage, political patronages, legacy support systems mingled with the new era of digital developments, media awareness, and shifting beliefs, values and aspirations.

I have always believed that India poses challenges for entrepreneurs that are significantly more complex, given its diversity and spread. It is also an outcome of the poor infrastructure, inefficient administration and regulatory framework, aided and abetted by local and regional, political alignments and agendas. Achieving success in these trying circumstances is a testimonial to their resolve and never-say-die attitude. There are clear learnings from their journeys, thoughts and actions, and should be viewed as such. The stories try and present the context and perspective of the varied challenges they surmount, and their day-to-day complexities and stress.

Each story attempts to demonstrate a few of these across states, sectors and industries, and in various stages of evolution of the business, straddling a unique set of regional, social and environmental nuances. There are no right or wrong approaches; the solution(s) some of the characters opt for are driven by their own value systems, social ethos, the context of their problems and the ground realities. Their journeys have great lessons for us. Some harsh, some pleasant, some tough and some downright sobering, but they tell us the truth about what it takes to be an entrepreneur and build an S&ME in this country.

The Hiring Dilemma

Deepak Sharma was lost in contemplation, wondering what had gone wrong in the plan to upgrade his organization and its capabilities. It had taken a lot of gumption, effort, cost and swallowing of pride to take that single momentous step to professionalize the organization and create management depth by inducting senior professionals into the primarily mom-and-pop set-up that he had started a few decades ago.

Deepak ran a successful medium enterprise, Flow Dynamics, in Mumbai. It specialized in flow and other measurement instruments for the process industry. Through hard work, developing long-lasting customer relationships, personal drive and integrity, and a focus on delivering value, he had built a healthy, growing and profitable business. His joint venture (JV) partner, a Canada-based global giant, was pleased with the venture and was pushing him to grow faster, expand to neighbouring geographies and establish a global manufacturing hub to leverage the cost arbitrage while taking advantage of the government's thrust on 'Make in India'.

Deepak Sharma had decided to bite the bullet but needed to infuse capital to make the transition from an owner, entrepreneur-driven boutique set-up to a professional and regionally significant company with a pan-Indian, multi-locational identity. The process of inducting a private equity player was in itself a tale to be told, but his current dilemma had arisen following this induction and needed to be resolved quickly, if the journey that he had begun a year earlier was to culminate in success.

His Board meeting that morning had not gone well. Mark Robertson, the representative of the Canadian partner and their global business leader, and Adil Jussawala, the private equity investor representative, had both been very hard on him. Two of his professional hires had decided to part ways with his company, and he was forced to justify the happening.

'This is clearly a case of poor anticipation, management and leadership,' Mark had stated.

They had both also emphasized the fact that the company could not continue to function in an ad hoc manner and that Deepak needed to fix this on a priority basis. This harsh feedback was in spite of the fact that in the quarter gone by, the company had demonstrated results that were head and shoulders above those of any other organization in the industry.

Deepak was at a loss as to why two of his marquee hires, the head of sales and the head of delivery, had decided to leave him and pursue their careers elsewhere. Deepak had spent considerable time and effort in wooing Amit and Aditya and convincing them to leave their lucrative multinational company jobs, offering them attractive packages including stature, role, compensation and considerable stock options. In fact, he had to work hard to convince his brother and wife, the two other shareholders in his company, to agree to hire Amit and Aditya.

What would he tell them now? That he had made a mistake in hiring professionals in an attempt to grow the company? His mentorship group had endorsed his views and had seconded his initiative unanimously. What would he tell them? That they had all been wrong? Deepak was struggling to understand what had gone wrong so he could restore confidence in his leadership capabilities. His pride had taken a beating as he had preened to all on being recognized as a good leader by both industry bodies and his Board.

He decided to reach out to his friend and confidante, Sakshi Malhotra, a seasoned professional who led a successful consulting firm and was a recognized authority on organizational strategy and sustainable growth. He had met Sakshi a few years ago and had come to value her advice on the various challenges he had faced. He had consciously set aside his male ego and had deferred to her better perspective, judgement and experience and had benefitted from it whenever he had done so.

They decided to meet for lunch at his club the next day.

After settling down, Sakshi asked, 'So Deepak, why so glum? You're looking stressed, and it seems you're struggling with something very serious.'

'Yes, I am,' Deepak immediately responded.

He then went on to brief her on the two senior professionals he had hired, their decision to exit and his struggle to identify what had caused them to leave and to figure out if he could fix it.

Sakshi heard him out, and then gently piped, 'I am going to summarize my thoughts on what could have caused the situation based on what you have told me, and knowing the two persons in this case. We can then explore ways, if any, of trying to salvage the situation. Would you like to take some notes, to help you assimilate this?'

Deepak's notes ran thus:

- The two professionals had come from a structured environment with strong processes and systems to an organization with no such structure and had struggled to deal with the chaos.
- There was no support system in Flow Dynamics in terms of market research, best practices, experienced people or large teams to assist the two gentlemen in growing the organization, both internally and externally.
- I did not provide budgetary support to either source this externally, or try and build systems internally. I merely hired them and then left them to it.
- I believed that they needed their space to perform and thus refrained from hand-holding or even providing key inputs and suggestions to help them adjust to the environment and thus be more effective in their roles.
- My propensity to step in and do the work myself when they struggled only made them feel more unwanted and undermined. Letting go is something I have to learn.
- Hiring the best from the industry cuts both ways. I need to seriously consider if Flow Dynamics needs that profile, and is it the best for the company at this stage in its growth journey? I must think in terms of 'fit for purpose'.
- One swallow does not make a summer. Having the best generals without the support team gets one nowhere. So, I must ensure that they have the basic support system

to do their jobs effectively.
- The rest of the organization needs to be sensitized as well. Resistance to change and the fear of outsiders is a company dynamic that I should have proactively anticipated and addressed.
- Organizational change is a multi-pronged, leader-driven process. I should have provided leadership with maturity to drive it. I should have stayed hands-on in this.

Deepak read and re-read his notes on his way back to the office. He could not disagree with any of Sakshi's observations. He marvelled at how he had been blind to these issues; indeed, now that Sakshi had articulated them, it sounded like common sense, which he should have easily seen.

He wondered if all entrepreneur-driven organizations, at some stage in their journey, were faced with this reality, and if they were, then what were the corrective actions that could be taken to undo some of the damage.

As he thought about the insights he had gained, the actions and steps he needed to take started crystallizing in his mind. He squared his shoulders, looked ahead with determination and renewed confidence, as he visualized a future for Flow Dynamics with renewed hope.

The Ca(sh)tch 22 Situation

Madhivannan and his finance manager were having their usual crisis conclave, which had become a big source of stress for the former. Apart from the routine business issues, Ramachandra Reddy, aka Ram, his finance manager, had recently been raising the constant bugbear of no cash to meet business expenses. The year had begun very well for Chennai Safety Engineers, or CSE, with a healthy order book and a long list of marquee clients signed up for projects for a couple of years ahead. The company had always been profitable, and the retained earnings had been completely used to fund growth over the past ten years.

Madhivannan, the founder and CEO of the successful CSE, an engineering company that specialized in the design, fabrication, erection and commissioning of safety systems for large manufacturing units, was scratching his head as to why, in spite of CSE being a profitable venture with strong customer references and a reputation for quality and timeliness, and with no bad debts, he was being bombarded on an almost daily basis by Ram for cash infusions to run the ship.

He decided to take the bull by the horns and confronted Ram.

'Why are we constantly hard up for cash? Don't we make money on every project and collect within the industry norms on all the projects? Where is the money going?'

Ram put a sheet a paper in front of him. 'Sir, these are the receipts and inflows this month, and these are the payments made. These are the payments that need to be made urgently, without which the projects will come to a standstill. This second sheet shows the same from April till date, including the cash we started the year with.'

Madhivannan studied the sheet carefully. The numbers looked fair, at a glance. The vendors identified as critical for payments were also above board, and the gap between cash available in the bank, and payments to be made was a good ₹2 crore. For a company that had a turnover of ₹45 crore, a pipeline of ₹100 crore and profit before tax of ₹6.5 crore, he was trying to comprehend how, in spite of retained earnings in cash of close to ₹5 crore the previous financial year, they were hard up for the same, two months into the new financial year.

'Let me go through this in detail, Ram,' he said to Reddy and walked into his cabin to carefully analyse the apparent anomaly. As he was studying the numbers, he was accosted by his projects and delivery head, Aditya, who further complicated matters by saying, 'Madhi, we need to take delivery of the imported components, and GST needs to be paid. Ram tells me there is no cash to do so. This could have serious repercussions on our delivery schedules and will lead to liquidity damages.'

Madhi responded: 'Yes, Aditya. Ram has raised the issue with me as well. He has also given me a cash flow statement, which is what I am grappling with. Give me today to figure it out. In the meanwhile, see what preparations you can make so we hit the ground running the moment the components are in.'

Madhi sat deep in thought. All possibilities crossed his mind. He started listing them out:

- Are we making extra payments to vendors?
- Are we losing cash on our projects? But the project profitability sheets show otherwise...
- We are making a margin of at least 25 per cent on every project. So where is the shortfall?
- Are we being swindled by employees? But Ram is a trusted and old employee, and only he and I authorize and sign payments.
- Are we not reporting collections correctly? But the accounting system shows otherwise, and all reconciliations are complete. Ram is a stickler for that.
- There are no cash payments, barring a few in very low amounts. So where is the leak?
- There have been no capital expenses. Everything is on lease or hire.
- We do not give loans to employees, barring a few advances against salaries, which are all approved by me.
- All suppliers are on letters of credit, or open credit terms, so there are no supplier advances.

It did not add up and Madhi was very worried as the numbers did not make sense. He quietly closed the door to his office and picked up the phone.

'Raman, I know I am infringing on your busy day, but I need to see you this evening. I am grappling with a very serious problem, which could derail CSE,' he blurted out as soon as his call was answered.

The voice at the other end confirmed, 'Sure Madhi. Let's catch up at the Chola Sheraton at 6 p.m. prior to my dinner engagement.'

Madhi had met Raman during a seminar at which the latter had delivered a sterling talk on entrepreneurship and its key challenges. Madhi had been very impressed and had, in fact, spent an additional week engaging with Raman to develop a growth strategy for CSE, which had paid off handsomely. This had further cemented their mentor-mentee relationship, and they had become good friends.

Madhi knew he needed to identify the root cause and find both a short-term and long-term solution to the problem. He had confidence in his mentor's ability to provide them, and he was all ears.

Raman walked into the coffee shop at exactly 6.00 p.m., as Madhi knew he would. This was one of the many things he admired and respected about Raman. Not one to waste time, Raman, after a brief exchange of pleasantries, got straight to the point.

'So what's giving you sleepless nights?' he asked.

Madhi walked Raman through the problem, his thoughts on the possibilities and his lack of success in pinpointing the root cause.

'Let me ask you a few questions, Madhi,' Raman said when Madhi had finished. 'Humour me and please answer them, no matter how irrelevant they may seem. I need to quickly arrive at the possible cause, and then we can explore short-term and long-term fixes.'

The following are the questions Raman asked:

- What was your turnover last year? What is it likely to be this year?
- How many of your earlier projects are yet to be commissioned?
- What is the value of transactions that are still under execution, and when do you see them reaching completion?
- Who decides the pricing for your projects, and the margins and profitability of each of them?
- What are your typical payment terms with your vendors and customers?
- What is the average value and days outstanding for debtors and creditors?
- What is the total corporate overhead of your company? What percentage of revenues is the overhead?
- Do you use bank lines for working capital? What are they?

Madhi's detailed answers demonstrated his intimate knowledge and awareness of everything that happened in CSE.

After Raman was done questioning him, Madhi asked, 'Don't you think there is a possibility of misappropriation here? You have not even considered that, Raman. That's on the top of my list.'

'Don't worry, let me think about what you've told me.' Raman read through the notes he had made as Madhi had been responding to his questions.

Then he started talking.

'You are growing at 40 per cent this year, and hence are projecting a revenue of ₹63 crore. Your projects are priced with a gross margin of 30 per cent and after corporate overheads, you will make a profit before tax of 18 per cent. Am I right?'

'Yes,' Madhi responded.

'So that means the cash required to conduct the business should be equivalent to at least four months of working capital, which translates to about ₹20 crore, Madhi. The same last year would have been ₹15 crore. The increase of ₹5 crore should have been met from your retained earnings. But you are claiming a shortfall of ₹2 crore in just two months.'

Raman continued, 'Madhi, your issue is twofold. As per your customer payment terms, you are paid 25 per cent of the value of the project on erection and commissioning and receive 10 per cent as a warranty and performance retention. The projects awaiting commissioning amount to almost ₹30 crore from last year, and hence 35 per cent is still unpaid. That in itself is ₹10.5 crore. You also have projects worth ₹15 crore that are under the performance warranty period. Ten per cent of that also remains unpaid. Hence the unpaid dues from earlier projects amount to about ₹12 crore, and you are currently executing projects worth ₹60 crore, for which you have been procuring materials, which will translate into payments for supply, which is only 50 per cent, along with the 15 per cent you received as mobilization earlier.

'This essentially means that every year, you have to find additional working capital, over and above the retained earnings, to fund the erection and commissioning, the warranties, the corporate overheads, the GST payments and the income tax liabilities. With a bottom line of 12 per cent, this translates to a requirement of at least 23 per cent, conservatively. It's a vicious circle...you will keep getting deeper into this problem as you go along,' Raman concluded.

'So what is the solution?' Madhi questioned.

'My recommendations would be the following. First, change your pricing to ensure your gross margins are always above the threshold of 35 per cent.

'Renegotiate the payment terms with your customers to ensure the erection and commissioning milestone payment is not greater than 15 per cent.

'Arrange for a bank line to include bank guarantees and letters of credit wherein you can issue letters of credit to your suppliers for credit periods of 120 days and bank guarantees for the warranty performance to customers. This will save you the cash, but cost you about 5 per cent per annum.

'In the short term, you need an overdraft from your banker, and then you may need to get a loan from a non-banking financial company to bridge the gap in the medium term.

'In the long term, better bank lines may not be possible without a capital infusion. You will need to raise capital by diluting your stake.

'For SMEs with long revenue cycles, cash flow planning is even more critical than profitability. Most of us do not connect pricing and profitability, with the hidden negative impact of large working capital cycles. So keep your eye on the cash flow projections going forward and plan for that more than budgeting for profitability,' Raman concluded as he finished his cup of filter coffee.

After Raman left, Madhivannan went through his notes again. He was chastened by the revelations and now appreciated Ram's subtle requests to look closely at pricing and commercial terms on every project before approving the financial bid. He rebuked himself for not having seen this earlier, but was grateful that he had someone like Raman as a sounding board.

He remembered tales of some of his acquaintances who had been forced to exit profitable and growing businesses in the safety engineering field, and now understood why. Cash is king, he concluded.

Capital Crimes

'I don't want anything to do with the business under the circumstances,' yelled Rekha before she walked out of Samir's office.

Samir was flabbergasted. They had been business partners for seven years and had created a successful data analytics company, which had grown from strength to strength to become recognized as one of the key players in the analytics field. Their domain expertise and technical competence were hailed by every customer, and they had rarely lost a client to anyone else.

All that had come to nought over the past six months, and Samir was at a loss as to how things had culminated in this acrimony between them. He was kicking himself for letting things move in this direction, albeit accepting that he had been manipulated by circumstances and the key new players in the fray. He resolved to reach out to his mentor, Dinesh, who was aware of the chain of events and had warned him to tread carefully. There was no time to be wasted.

'Hi, Samir, what's up? It's been a while since I heard from you,' said Dinesh when he heard Samir on the other end of the line.

Samir came straight to the point, 'I need to meet you as soon as possible. Can I send you a ticket for tomorrow morning's flight to Bengaluru?'

Samir's urgency and underlying fear were not missed by Dinesh, who had built a successful business as a mentor to SMEs over the past decade by hand-holding them through moments of uncertainty and aiding them in successfully navigating pitfalls. He agreed.

'I'll brief you when we meet, Dinesh,' Samir said before hanging up.

He then hurried to find Rekha, with whom he needed to have a heart to heart talk as he knew that without their partnership, this company, Analytics Inc., would go nowhere at all. They had been colleagues at a large multinational firm operating in the analytics domain before they had decided to set up a boutique outfit in Bengaluru. He fondly remembered how he had asked Rekha to be the CEO, and he himself had taken on the role of the COO. Their complementary skills in business development and sales, and technology and delivery had dovetailed to create a beautiful and successful partnership.

Unfortunately, it had all fallen apart over the last six months. His thoughts went back to that fateful day when Rekha had walked into his cabin and announced, 'We have a once in a lifetime opportunity to cross the hump and become a multinational company!'

Intrigued, Samir had asked Rekha to tell him more. They had stepped out to the nearest Starbucks as they did not want any of the other staff members to overhear their conversation, the nature of which was sensitive.

A few months earlier to this, they had both accepted the fact that they needed to infuse capital into the business in order to continue growing and began actively searching for a strategic or financial investor under the guidance of Dinesh.

The search had started with a lot of excitement. Several fund houses, large IT companies and a smattering of high net worth individuals had expressed their willingness to look at the possibility of investing in Analytics Inc. Dinesh, who was guiding Samir and Rekha through the fundraising process, had sifted through the list of potential investors and had recommended a few with whom they should move ahead to the next level.

Then, the story had turned. Rekha and Samir had diverse views on what constituted a fair valuation for the infusion of equity capital, and who should be the chosen contenders. This chalk and cheese dilemma, could not be bridged, even with the best efforts of Dinesh, whom they both respected. Rekha was of the opinion that the company should get multiples on revenue in excess of six, while Samir had stayed pragmatic and reasoned that given the slowdown in the global economy, a four times multiple on the previous fiscal year's revenues would be a fair value to go ahead with. They had argued, coaxed, cajoled, debated and sought diverse opinions, but the deadlock could not be broken.

'I think you guys are being unrealistic,' Dinesh had cautioned. 'In the current scenario, even a product company should not expect a six times multiple on the top line.'

Rekha's response had been to state, 'In that case, I do not want to bring in an investor right now. Let's keep looking till someone matches the price.'

Samir, though disagreeing with her, had decided to accept her decision. They had dropped their various suitors and had returned to focusing on the business of growing and expanding. Shortly after, Rekha had left for the UK on a business development visit and to attend the Annual Analytics Conclave that was being held there.

It was when Rekha had returned from the UK, that she had dropped her bombshell as they both sat in Starbucks. She told Samir what had transpired while she was in the UK.

'I had a discussion with Advanced Analytics & Intelligence, the large UK-based MNC, and the firm has expressed a desire to look at us for an investment in the future, when we are a US $3 million revenue company. I think we are a couple of years away. We should cultivate them consciously.' She went on to add, 'Tom Mascarenhas, their strategy head and the deputy MD, had a private chat with me. He believes that the pitch to acquire Analytics Inc, is a distinct play, which he plans to exploit, and maybe eighteen months away. He has offered to get his friend to invest in us immediately, which can then take us through till the acquisition deal matures, and is actioned. What do you think, Samir?'

Samir had liked the idea, but wanted to delve further. 'Is there a catch here that I am not able to understand? Am I missing something?' he had asked, ever the cautious one.

'Let's step out for lunch,' Rekha had suggested, and they had both gone to a nearby restaurant specializing in Bengali cuisine.

Over lunch, she had elaborated on Tom's proposal. 'Tom wants to get his friend to put in half a million US dollars through one of his investment companies, but is seeking a valuation of one and a half times the revenue for the last financial year. This is significantly lower than what I had in mind,' she had outlined. 'But, there are serious benefits. We will get a major share of all the sub-contract work from Advanced Analytics, which will help us scale up to a revenue greater than what we can achieve on our own. Apart from that, he has offered to pay us for a secondary dilution of half the amount. Hence US $250,000 out of the US $500,000 will come to us, which we could never expect on any of the deals we have discussed. That's the biggest kicker!' she had emphasized, her excitement showing through.

Samir remembered that he had, even then, cautioned, 'I hope we are doing the right thing by tying ourselves to Tom and his friend, as well as wedding our strategy with Advanced Analytics. Can we at least sleep on this for a few days before we get back to Tom?'

Rekha had been adamant.

'We need to give Tom an answer by tomorrow. He wants to move ahead quickly on this as his friend is making a few other investments in India and wants to close all of them with one visit,' she had countered.

They had agreed to call Dinesh to discuss the matter later in the day, after the rest of the staff had left so they could speak with minimal risk of being overheard.

Dinesh had asked them a series of questions to help them think through the proposal:

- How well did they know Tom? Could they depend on him to follow through with his offer?
- Was there a risk of interested party transaction complaints or questions?
- Why was Tom pushing the deal through in a hurry?
- How did his friend's company plan to get involved with

the acquisition? Would it play an operating role?
- Would the acquiring company hold any Board positions, or have a say in day-to-day operations?
- Were the other acquisitions being finalized by Tom's friend in similar domains? Were they in Bengaluru?
- Who were the founders of the other companies that were being acquired, and could Rekha and Samir reach out to them to know more about their business and synergies with Analytics Inc?
- Did the acquiring firm plan to let Analytics Inc. continue to run the way it was? Or did they have a different game plan?
- Was the firm cleared to invest in India? Did they meet the Foreign Exchange Regulation Act (FERA) and the Foreign Exchange Management Act (FEMA) regulations?
- Had Rekha and Samir discussed the roadmap for the future with the acquiring firm? Was there a meeting of minds on the overall approach and synergy in thought?
- Had Rekha and Samir considered the implications of the secondary dilution? With it, they would be giving away a significant portion of their company. Did they want to do that?

They were all very valid and pertinent questions, Samir now realized, which they should have paid attention to. But the euphoria of immediate investment, some money in the bank for themselves, and the thought of an assured acquisition a few years down the road had made them blind to the obvious red flags and they had decided to accept Tom's proposal. *Hindsight is always 20-20*, thought Samir.

Today's outburst from Rekha marked a culmination of

the months of stress and conflict that had ensued after the investment company, London Creek, had finalized its investment. A memorandum of understanding had been signed, which had to be translated into a shareholders agreement within sixty days. The transfers took place post-haste, and then came the first signs of problems. Before the agreement was signed, Tom shared that his friend, Jose, would be in India to review all his investments. The other investments Jose was making were all in Bengaluru-based companies.

The visit was uneventful, except for the fact that Jose had been accompanied by two gentlemen, the head of strategy and the CFO of London Creek. The apparent purpose of their visit was so that they could get to know the management teams of the various companies they were investing in. The visit was followed by a conference call, during which was laid out the reporting relationship between Analytics Inc. and the two gentlemen who had visited the country. It came as a surprise, as their understanding with Tom was a Board Engagement and no oversight by anyone else. Samir and Rekha had taken it in their stride, but things did not end there.

A few weeks later a strategy call was held, during which there was talk of merging the three investments into one company. The condition for the merger was that Samir would be the CEO of the combined entity and Rekha would be the head of sales and business development for the common venture. They had both shot that down, and things had died down for a while. Then a few weeks later Jose had politely read them the riot act. They had had no choice but to agree to the merger, and Jose had very graciously given them three months to comply.

Today marked the end of the three-month period. Hence, Rekha's outburst. Samir knew that they had to get out of the jam and hoped Dinesh would have a solution. He did not want to leave Rekha out of what they had created together; it was as much hers as his. He also knew that their complementary skills were needed to make Analytics Inc. a force to be reckoned with.

The next day dawned bright and sunny and Samir smiled, hoping the day would be as bright for them. Dinesh was on his way from the airport and both Rekha and Samir were eagerly waiting for him.

Dinesh came straight to the point. 'Let's not dwell on whose fault it is, and why you went ahead with the deal. If both of you agree that it is a poor deal and is not worth moving ahead with, then let us send a notice of termination. I understand that no agreement has been signed and the MOU is no longer valid. There is the added complication of FERA and FEMA and RBI approvals for returning the unsubscribed capital money.'

'It's more than that,' Rekha chipped in. 'We cannot pay back the money as we have used it in the company, and personally used it to acquire assets.'

This put Dinesh in deep thought. After an uncomfortable silence, he said, 'Here's what I am going to ask you to do. Only this time, please follow my advice to the T.

'First, speak to Jose and tell him that no changes can be made till the agreement is signed and that the RBI is asking questions. He has to provide an explanation as to why the documentation and supporting evidence required to sign the agreement have not been completed. Once that is done, you will have to sign an extension of the MOU, or a fresh one, before you can go ahead with the agreement.

'If he is not willing to provide the relevant details of his company ownership and as a legal and compliant entity as the investment was made by the company, then a document cancelling the arrangement will need to be recorded, with the stipulation that the money will be returned, without any interest, within a period of two years, and the same is to be submitted to the RBI, for their approval. If this is acceptable, which it should be to Tom and Jose, given the fact that they are the ones who have delayed this, we should be able to close this out within thirty days.

'I think we will be able to get out of this,' Dinesh opined.

Rekha and Samir were both left spellbound and realized the value of Dinesh's experience and maturity. They were humbled and in awe of him as they escorted him to the taxi waiting to take him to the airport.

The same thought crossed both their minds simultaneously. There are no free lunches, and all capital comes with its share of challenges.

Taxing Times

Soumik Banerjee sat outside the income tax commissioner's office, a worried look on his face. His company, Electrical Design Engineers, had been found guilty of tax evasion in the previous financial years. All the appeals and recourse options had been exhausted, and this was the day of reckoning, when the company would have to accept its total liability and figure out where to raise the amount for the payment that had to be deposited within forty-eight hours.

Soumik was there as the founder and MD of the business to accept the final liability and to try to convince the commissioner of the above-board credentials of the business he had built. The ramshackle office, the creaking wooden bench and the humid Kolkata weather did nothing to boost his spirits. His friend, chartered accountant and auditor, Janardhan Poojari, sat next to him, going through the documents in an oversized box file, a collection of all the letters, evidence and explanations that had been produced in the past in an attempt to absolve the company from the accusation of deliberate obfuscation of income.

While waiting for the commissioner, A.K. Das, to give him an audience, Soumik went over, for the umpteenth time, the chain of events that had resulted in him warming the bench outside the commissioner's door today. It had begun about thirty months ago, when Poojari had come into his office with a demand that they restate their books of accounts.

'Don't pay so much income tax,' was his plea. 'Why give hard-earned money to the government? Are you running a charity? Let's book a few more expenses and reduce the company's tax liability.'

After hearing him out, Soumik, who was far from convinced about the legalities of the suggestion, had responded, 'Janardhan, let's not do anything that is illegal or unethical. I am an honest, god-fearing, educated engineer-businessman, and I do not want to do something that I have never done in my life!'

However, Poojari was a true-blue chartered accountant and had a ready answer for this. 'You are not doing anything wrong,' he had insisted. 'You are only showing extra purchases, which will be against valid bills that I will procure for you. And let us increase your and your brother's salaries for the year by 25 per cent, and that will suffice. Our tax liability will be reduced by fifty lakh!'

Soumik's elder brother was also a director of the company and was drawing a salary, though he was not involved in the day-to-day workings of EDE.

Soumik now regretted the fact that he had shown weakness and uncertainty then, which Poojari had taken as an acceptance of the suggestion.

Things had moved quickly after that. The bills for the

purchase of steel sheets for the fabrication of electrical panels were procured from Bose Traders through Poojari's good offices, and the compensation for both Soumik and his brother was increased, thus reducing profits before tax by ₹1.5 crore and saving the company almost ₹50 lakh in taxes in the bargain.

Soumik had forgotten all about the incident until his accountant, Shubra, came to him almost three years later and said, 'We have got a sales tax enquiry seeking details on the purchase of steel from Bose Traders three years ago. We have to produce the original bills and delivery challans for the purchases for the sales tax office by tomorrow.'

'We do not buy steel from Bose Traders, as far as I remember,' Soumik had responded. 'But check with purchase if we have ever dealt with Bose Traders. Go through our audited files and pull out the purchase bills and delivery proofs. Also, take the stock register copy to show the receipt entry as further proof.'

He was fairly confident that the value system he had consciously cultivated in the organization would have ensured that record-keeping and documentation would be complete and fail-safe.

Two weeks later, Shubra had made another appearance in his cabin as Soumik was wrapping up a very satisfying sales review. Soumik's spirits had been high as the numbers were very heartening.

'The sales tax authorities are here to investigate tax evasion by us. They claim we have accounted for fake bills and want proof of purchase and other details on some steel purchases made from Bose Traders. You remember we spoke about this issue a couple of weeks ago?' Shubra asked.

'Yes, I remember. Did you find all the documents I had

asked you to collect? Show them the paperwork', Soumik said.

Shubra was back in ten minutes.

'They want to meet you, and they have evidence that the bills are false. It seems that Bose Traders are not steel merchants, and they have accepted that these were false bills raised by them.'

Soumik remembered the discussion with Poojari and asked Shubra to contact Janardhan and ask him to come to the office immediately. It was fortunate that his office was only a few streets away.

Janardhan and he had met the sales tax inspectors. They had come prepared with all the documentation and evidence and the statement from Bose Traders, and it was evident that there was no way out but to pay the penalty and clear the liability. Soumik had reconciled to the fact that by paying a tax and penalty of ₹11 lakh they had still managed tax savings of around ₹50 lakh. Though mentally, he ticked himself off for acting foolishly and accepting Janardhan's suggestion.

But things had not ended there. The bigger bombshell came three weeks later. Shubra was once again the bearer of the news.

'We have received an income tax notice for tax evasion and false returns. The same year and the same Bose Traders transaction are under question.' She proudly stated.

'Ask Poojari to respond to the notice and handle the situation,' Soumik had responded and then forgotten about it.

Then started the communication war. Letters to and fro, meetings with the deputies in the tax office, Poojari and his constant requests for meetings and time for discussions, all at the expense of business growth and running the company. The matter had gone to the tribunal, and EDE had lost the appeal. Following this, a demand for ₹1.25 crore as tax plus penalty had landed on Soumik's desk. He had had no choice but to get Poojari to set up a meeting with the commissioner so he could seek to settle the claim at the earliest.

'Mr Das will see you now,' the peon announced, bringing Soumik back to the present. What had started as an attempt to pay lower taxes had snowballed into a long-drawn exercise, costing time and a great deal more money than the proclaimed savings, not to mention the mental trauma that he was going through. It wasn't over yet, was his last thought as he entered Mr Das's chamber.

'As a bhadralok, how can you do this, Mr Banerjee?' was Mr Das's first statement. 'Your company has never been scrutinized as we thought you were an honest taxpayer. We will now have to relook at all your returns.'

'Sir, we are honest people and it was a one-time mistake made by us. Please treat us as such,' Soumik made an earnest plea.

Tea arrived, and the discussion continued well into the lunch hour. It finally ended with Mr Poojari submitting the challan for the tax and penalty paid as per the ruling.

Mr Das's parting shot was, 'I hope I never see you here again, Mr Banerjee!'

As they left the offices of the income tax commissioner, Soumik suggested to Poojari that they grab a bite at a nearby restaurant. During lunch, he could hold himself back no longer. He decided to give Janardhan a piece of his mind, albeit accepting guilt first:

'Poojari, I think we should get out of this mindset of trying to avoid paying taxes at all cost. See where it has got us. I accept that I was the one who agreed to this, but as my friend and financial advisor, I think you should keep me on the right path. Your role has to be one of a guide and mentor, ensuring we always do what is ethical and above board in our financial and business dealings.

'As we grow, we will become more visible, noticed and watched more than ever for our business practices, by our suppliers, customers, employees and well-wishers. I do not want our reputation to be tarnished because of such folly. I have been getting feelers from private equity funds that are interested in investing in us, and one of the questions they have asked me is if the company has any cases pending against it from the tax authorities. I will have to walk them through this one if I decide to move ahead, but it will result in a residual doubt in their minds as to whether there are any more such hidden litigations or contingent liabilities.'

He had heard all this at a seminar on compliance that he had attended a few weeks ago, and all those pointers were coming back to him. Soumik was actually castigating himself for bringing EDE so close to being branded a dubious organization for life, after twenty-five long years of an untarnished history.

Debts And Don'ts

Anjali Deshmukh sat with a troubled look on her face, trying to unravel the intricacies of financial management and leveraging. As the CFO, albeit underqualified for the position as she herself was the first to admit, she was contending with the organization's need for financing to enable and support the path of rapid growth that the owner of the company, Mr Kishore Ranade, was pursuing. Her dilemma was how to determine what was prudent and how to draw the line on leverage such that it did not compromise the long-term health and viability of the organization.

Kishore's company, One Up Communications, a niche player in the communications technology space, had hit an upward surge a few years ago and had continued to ride the wave. It had become a successful and profit-making organization with an enviable list of blue-chip clients. As part of the journey to scale, Anjali had been instrumental in securing bank lines and alternative debt lines to support this endeavour. She had read about and heard an eminent speaker talk about financial leverage and its benefits for a profit-making company, and had promptly explored the option of seeking working capital support from a large private sector bank, one of the biggest in the banking sector.

One thing had led to another, and the relationship with the bank had grown from strength to strength, driven primarily by her ability to meet the demands of the bank and convince Kishore to accept their terms and conditions for continued support and enhancement of lines. In the process, the company had secured an A1 credit rating from a leading credit rating agency, albeit incurring a significant cost on an ongoing basis, year on year. Anjali had also reached out to a few non-banking financial companies (NBFC) as the firm's cash flow requirements were skewed and financial year-ends called for a surge in cash availability, which the bank did not recognize or support.

In spite of her achievements, Anjali felt inadequate and struggled to understand completely the nuances and market dynamics of the debt and banking space. She had kept her concerns to herself, but she was now coming to realize that she did need help, and she wanted to discuss the same with Kishore. Being a person of action, she walked up to Kishore's cabin and knocked.

'Come in Anjali, what's up? Any new fires?' Kishore enquired.

'No, I want to pick your brain on something. Do you have ten minutes?' she countered.

Kishore was very perceptive. He could read her uncertainty and sensed that she was struggling with something. He decided to drop everything and chat with her to try and unravel the reason for her worry. Anjali needed no urging. She quickly took him through the concerns and doubts she had regarding the size of the company's debt burden, its costs, the regulatory and documentation requirements, and her own inability to add value to the whole process, given her limited knowledge and exposure to treasury as a specific area of her role. Kishore knew he had put her loyalty and integrity above her qualifications for executing the larger role he had thrust on her, thus literally putting her in a corner, which was now manifesting itself as self-doubt.

'I am guilty of thrusting too much responsibility on you without giving you the exposure and perspective you need to effectively execute your role. Unfortunately, I myself do not have the expertise to add value in this space. But, I have a dear friend and advisor, Mr Harjeet Singh, who is a seasoned banker and now advises SMEs on financial management, capital structuring and capital raising. He is the best person to guide us; I can engage him to take us through these trying times, and handhold our finance function especially, on our road to growth and expansion.'

Anjali was relieved. She was more than happy to take advice from an experienced professional, and she started putting together a list of her doubts, questions and clarifications.

The following morning, Harjeet arrived at the One Up Communications offices to meet with Anjali and Kishore. A tall, distinguished gentleman with a greying beard, and sporting a sombre black turban and rimless glasses, he looked the picture of an erudite professor walking into a class of enthusiasts.

He got down to business quickly. 'Kishore, I need information on what you have been doing for leveraging and borrowings so that I am up to speed. I am going to ask a few questions and will need the answers before I can advise you on the right course of action for the company.'

'Definitely, Harjeet. Anjali is our CFO, and she will have all the answers for you. I may not have complete information on the subject,' Kishore quickly responded.

Harjeet's questions ran like this:

- What is the exposure, in terms of sanctioned limits and utilized limits, for both fund-based and non-fund-based limits?
- How many banks does the company have this total line from?
- How often are the limits revalidated? What is the cost of borrowing, fee structure and review fees being paid by the company?
- What was the company's last credit rating, and does the bank specify whether they have looked at it before giving an interest rate for the borrowing?
- What margin money is the company paying for non-fund-based limits?
- Are cash flows skewed, and do they have significant peaks and troughs? How do you tide over these?
- Does the company have other NBFC loans? At what cost and fee structures?
- What is the revenue run rate, and what is the position on debtors and creditors?
- What are the margins on the earnings before interest, taxes, depreciation and amortization (EBITDA), and what is the profit before tax?
- What directors' liability policies has the company taken, if any?

- What collateral has been offered to the banks?

Anjali had all the answers as well as supporting documentation detailing various transactions. Harjeet Singh recorded each of her responses and then asked for a few minutes to study the documents she had provided.

There was a period of expectant silence, broken only by the humming of Kishore's air-conditioner and the nervous drumming of his fingers on his desk. Finally, after a long drawn period of silence, Harjeet said, 'Kishore, I am going to talk about some of the traps you have been drawn into, and the ways out from them. If you follow my advice, you will keep One Up Communications away from the debt trap you are being pulled into.

'Let me elaborate:

'You have a debt burden of ₹12 crore on a funded basis for a company with a turnover of ₹20 crore. This is neither advisable nor sustainable. The cost of debt itself is taking away 8 per cent from your profitability, which is not tenable in the long run.

'This is without the additional burden of non-fund-based limits of ₹6 crore, and the margin money of 50 per cent, which is effectively costing you an additional 2 per cent of your profits. Thus, you are eating away 10 per cent of your margins.

'You have also been forced to take a directors' liability insurance policy and a life protection policy. This adds another ₹25 lakh to your expenses every year.

'The processing fees for the renewal of your limits with the bank and the NBFC fees are costing you another 1 per cent of the total debt. If I add all of this up, you are being charged about 13 per cent on your revenues. On a 25 per cent gross margin business, this makes little sense.

'What I would do immediately is the following:

- When dealing with banks, as in dealing with suppliers or customers, it is important to ensure you have at least two bankers. It diversifies risk. Don't you do it consciously for customers and suppliers? Why not for bankers!
- By doing so, you are increasing your negotiating powers. You will be able to obtain better and lower interest rates, lower margin monies, lower fees for trade facilities and more. It will also allow you to breathe easy. No single banker will be able to stifle you. Your current rates are far above what an A1-rated company should pay.
- Although you do not have an investor at present, at some point you will infuse private equity via a financial investor or a strategic one. They will see this as poor fiscal competence.
- Unsecured NBFC loans seem attractive, but they never are. They take away cash every month, but do not translate into expenses on your P&L. They are cash draining but not profit gaining, as only the interest payment can be expensed. So, see how quickly you can unwind them.
- You have skewed cash flows; there are months when your inflows are higher than the outflows. Create fixed deposits and take loans against them. They look better on your balance sheet and cost only 2 per cent more than the FD interest rates, at best. It will be significantly lower than your working capital cost. This will also allow you flexibility and speed in terms of getting it done.

'Be smart and use financial leverage to give you a kicker in terms of profit genuinely; but don't allow the debt merchants to get the kicker for themselves,' he summed up with a twinkle in his eye.

Both Anjali and Kishore nodded, definitely wiser, and now armed with some clear action points that they could immediately get going on.

Growth Pangs

Edward Sequira entered the boardroom a chastened man, fully aware that during the next three hours, the entire Board would be, in unison, singing one song: 'We told you so'. He was here to accept the responsibility for his ill-considered decision. He knew that he and the organization, which was already suffering the consequences of that decision, would have to work twice as hard to recover from the effects of his blunder.

His thoughts went back in time to another Board meeting, where he had first spoken about his idea. He recalled the proceedings clearly. On that fateful day eighteen months ago, the chairman of the Board, Mr Iyer, had been the voice of sanity and caution on behalf of the Board. But although his opinions had registered with Edward, he had failed to appreciate their purport.

Edward and his organization, HR & People Maestros, a human resources and people management company, had, after forty long years in the business, decided to pursue an aggressive growth path. Their expansion had been largely conceptualized, driven and led by Edward, who had taken over the reins of the business about two years prior and was convinced that there was an opportunity to take the business to a scale that would place it amongst the top twenty-five players in the world in its space. The Southeast Asian market presented the right opportunity given its similarities to India, including the robust growth in banking, financial services, telecom and retail.

As the MD and CEO, Edward had also pushed his belief that this growth had to be through inorganic means, as organic growth would limit the scale and rate of growth achievable. His efforts had led to the rapid expansion of branches, distribution points and liaison offices in some of the other countries. As part of his growth initiative, he had also actively participated in regional and international seminars and marketing events so he could seek out similar-minded individuals and explore companies that he could buy and integrate into HR & People Maestros.

During the course of this journey, about eighteen months ago, he had met Mark Rutherford and Phillip Tyler, two British nationals who had set up a boutique venture based out of Hong Kong with a small presence in Singapore as well. He had interacted with them in similar forums earlier, but this one had a purpose. He had broached the topic of an acquisition at a cocktail event in Singapore, and both Mark and Phil had jumped at it. One thing had led to another, and Edward had returned to India excited and convinced that he had his first acquisition target in the bag.

However, a serious challenge lay ahead. Edward was well aware that it would take all his skills and business knowledge, backed by substantial data to convince his Board that the opportunity made sense for their organization and that People Tech, the company that Mark and Phil ran, would be a good strategic acquisition. He now remembered that fateful day and the prolonged Board meeting that had taken place.

He had put forward a strong and passionate plea, quoting data from Hewitt, Aon and other research agencies on the growth of the managed human resources and people services market, the regional shares, the list of key players and how each of them had Southeast Asia as a key building block of their overall global strategy. His arguments were based on the following data points:

- People Tech was a young company, but had made significant inroads into the Hong Kong market.
- It was a profit-making company, and had been so for three years.
- Mark and Phillip were professionals, with over fifteen years of experience each, and knew this business well.
- They had a small team, and hence integration and assimilation would be easier.
- People Tech was the right-sized company with which to start an inorganic growth initiative.
- Both Mark and Phillip were UK nationals, which would give HR & People Maestros the much-needed international leadership team positioning.

He had also emphasized that he himself would drive the assimilation and growth of the company, together with Mark and Phillip.

He had then presented the due diligence reports and the legal opinions of the leading agencies he had drawn upon, as added comfort for the Board. At the end of his hour-long presentation, Edward had thought it had all gone fairly well. His team was eagerly waiting to hear the outcome of the deliberations and had plans for an evening of celebrations at their favourite pub if all went according to plan.

Mr Iyer had broken the silence after the presentation with a few very pertinent observations.

'People Tech seems to be focused on the mom-and-pop businesses and at the lower end of the market. I do not think that is what we should be looking for. The synergies may end up being non-existent.

'Further, the two gentlemen have never worked with large corporates and multinational companies. It may turn out to be too big a shift for them in terms of who they will have to deal with.

'Their business processes and documentation seem very rudimentary. This may lead to a change management situation, which may be too much for them to handle if they have to integrate with our strong processes and documentation culture.

'Their financials, though healthy, are largely based on cash payments and collections. It's on a rudimentary Excel accounting, and the due diligence reports clearly state this. Unresolved issues may therefore surface later.

'Do we know if they have made commitments on shares, sweat equity or employee stock ownership plans to any of their employees? There is normally a propensity to do so in such circumstances.

'I see that you are planning to provide a secondary dilution to the promoters to the tune of a million dollars each, and there is very little by way of capital that will be infused into the company. This means we will have to put in working capital to enable growth.

'Do we know what compensation both the co-founders are drawing, if any? If not, then the profitability is an inflated number. We need to replace it with the actual cost that we would be incurring if we went ahead with the merger.

'Our systems and software may necessitate a capital cost outlay, and we need to bake that into our costs and hence the break-even and recovery of investment. Do we have an estimate?

'Given these concerns and questions, I am not convinced there are synergies in this acquisition; is it a potential white elephant, and will it be something we will regret later?' Mr Iyer had said in conclusion.

Edward had pushed back and stated that he would personally ensure all these valid points were addressed and that the transaction was conducted with full awareness and appreciation of the challenges.

Today, eighteen months later, it had all come back to bite him, and he was left with no choice but to apprise the Board of the difficult decision he had arrived at and accept the responsibility for the monumental failure and significant write-off he was now proposing. Every one of the points made by Mr Iyer on that fateful day eighteen months ago had turned out to be prophesies.

The sequence of events had unfolded exactly as foretold. After about a month, Edward had realized that:

People Tech had no access to corporates. It was a mom-and-pop outfit. Hence, all business development required someone from Mumbai to travel and do the legwork, as well as introduce Mark and Phil. The synergies were indeed non-existent.

The two gentlemen were like fish out of water when dealing with MNCs. Their 'hi pal' backslapping approach did not go down well with the clients. Not only that, Edward's own team found them difficult to deal with. Even after repeated efforts by Edward, they seemed immune to any attempts to integrate with the corporate culture.

The attempt to introduce HR & People Management processes and systems had backfired and had been deliberately sabotaged, according to Edward, by the two gentlemen. It was a case of turf protection and resistance to change at its worst.

To add to this, Edward's finance team discovered bills from suppliers that had not been cleared for eight months. Neither Mark nor Phil professed any knowledge of these bills, nor did they offer an apology. The unpaid dues had made the deal non-viable and had pushed break-even to ten years.

That was not all. The head of People Tech's Singapore office produced a document, signed by both gentlemen, promising him 10 per cent sweat equity, which was due to him before the dilution and stake sale. Again, the two gentlemen glossed over this as a miss or slip up.

The secondary dilution and the cash flows after the discovery of the unpaid dues had resulted in a working capital infusion of almost US $1 million. Edward had had to borrow on the parent Indian company account to infuse the same, as his secondary dilution had made them the majority stakeholders, and the Hong Kong bankers would have nothing to do with it.

Both Mark and Phil had budgeted their salaries at US $150,000 each per annum, with 90 per cent as fixed costs in the operating plan for the year. Edward had accepted the plan at face value; probably the only time he had ever done such a thing.

He had then re-examined People Tech's accounts from the previous year and found that they had paid themselves only

US$ 30,000 each per annum earlier. They had ensured their stated profits for the year on which the acquisition was based, was inflated, by keeping their own costs low. Thus the profits, restated with this compensation, were actually a loss of US $50,000. Edward kicked himself for failing to get into the details.

The only saving grace was that there was no capital outlay for the new systems. Edward had decided to accept responsibility and live with the consequences, a write-off of about US $2.5 million. It was an expensive lesson in inorganic growth. He swore to himself that all future growth would happen only organically.

Such growth would definitely be slower, but it would also be significantly less risky. Further, any future acquisitions would only be done after they had created a provision for the risk. How he would do that was a different story.

Greed Expectations

Arun sat stunned: his mind had stopped functioning for a moment as he digested, or attempted to digest, what he had just heard and seen. He had heard a very loud horn and had seen a Rolls Royce Phantom drive through the gates of the famous Price Towers. Mr Govardhan Gupta sat pompously in the rear seat, grinning from ear to ear at the acquisition of his new toy. His young brat pup, Pantaki Gupta, or 'the Punk' as he liked to call himself, sat next to the driver and waved to Arun.

'Arun, let's go for a ride bro,' he declared. 'Dad is going to be in the office for at least a few hours, and we can do a couple of rounds of Noida till then. Shamsher will drive us!'

Not left with much of a choice, Arun slid quietly into the seat Gupta senior had vacated, with the Punk sliding in next to him. Govardhan Gupta waved the boys on, delight barely hidden on his face as he watched his two prized possessions exit the gates of Price Towers. As the car zipped through the various happening sectors of Noida, Arun could not help but reflect upon how his life had been transformed during the past six months.

Arun Kumar was from a lower-middle class family. He had lived all his life in a Railway Colony. He had worked his way through an engineering degree at one of India's premier institutes, NIT Rourkela, and had topped it with an MBA from IMT Ghaziabad.

He had graduated in 2009, a year when the placement scene had not been very promising. However, he was fortunate to have had the Punk as a classmate. He and the Punk had become close thanks to Arun's notes and consistently high CGPAs. Arun had always thought that the Punk had befriended him in the hope that some of Arun's intelligence and hardworking ethic would rub off on him, but the brat was too lazy and dumb to change.

As it turned out, the Punk spoke very highly of Arun to Gupta senior, and based on his darling boy's recommendations, Mr Gupta had offered Arun a very handsome salary, and a car to boot, to be part of his real estate start-up venture. Arun Kumar had thus entered the corporate world, a dork and a naïve kid who had visions of making his mark in the industry, the real estate sector, which, as they had learnt at IMT, was unorganized and on the cusp of professionalizing. Needless to say, Punk was also one of the four MBA graduates who was inducted into the fledgeling company.

The early days were a whirlwind of learning and late hours, interspersed with visits to the various watering holes in the National Capital Region (NCR). Arun had learnt how land was acquired as a first process of creating a real estate project. It was also a default option, as the Guptas were essentially land acquirers who had helped the doyens of the industry in

Noida to aggregate land parcels and then convert them into gated communities for residences or commercial exploitation. Agricultural land, wasteland, traditional family heirloom land and some political bonanzas were aggregated and converted to non-agricultural, commercially exploitable parcels.

The four recruits had been put under Mr Upadhyay who had explained what an acre, hectare and other units of area were. They also had classroom-like sessions with Mr Sunil Mathur, who was an ex-chief operating officer of a very large player in real estate and who had been entrusted with their education and grooming.

It was during this early period that Arun's first tryst with values verses value took place. An innocuous question posed to Mr Upadhyay had got him a response that stunned him.

He had asked, 'If we are buying parcels at ₹60,000 to ₹1 lakh per acre, then why are we valuing them at ₹20 lakh per acre in our books?'

To which the response had been, 'There is a cost of conversion, and we have incurred that cost. Hence, our land is now valued at ₹20 lakh per acre. This is the norm in the industry.'

'But aren't we overstating this cost? I remember Mr Sunil telling us that the typical cost of conversion is not greater than 200 per cent of the value of the land purchased, at its worst,' Arun had countered.

'Value needs to be created, boy! This is how real estate value is created,' had been the cryptic response.

However, Arun thought the sentiment reeked of greed and had vowed to take it up with Sunil Mathur the next day.

He had confronted Sunil the following day with the question. Sunil, in his laconic style, had quipped, 'Valuation is driven by expectations, greed expectations.'

Thus began Arun's education in the business dynamics of the real estate sector, a journey where he was now at a crossroads and had to choose the path he would travel on.

At the time, however, Arun had not probed further and got involved in learning the intricacies of designing gated communities, studying everything from solid waste treatment plants to power standby plants, from access roads to safety and security systems. He also learnt how to evaluate and shortlist vendors for the various construction processes and the project management team.

Then came the time of reckoning. It started with the application for the bank project finance. Gupta senior had involved him and the Punk in the negotiations with the bank.

'Our land bank is 150 acres and is valued at ₹33 crore. Hence, we are seeking ₹75 crore, which is a little less than 70 per cent of the total project cost of ₹110 crore,' Mr Govardhan Gupta told the bank.

Arun could not believe his ears. That is when the answer to the question of why the overvaluation, dawned on him. So here was the connect and the *leverage of greed into further expectations*, he thought to himself.

The general manager of the bank, which was a large public-sector undertaking, politely nodded and then said, 'Guptaji, the processing fees will be 1 per cent, and I would also like a private word with you as we go to see our ED.'

Saying this, he walked out with Gupta senior, who turned and winked at his son conspiratorially.

Pantaki later revealed to Arun that there was a 'facilitation fee' of 1.5 per cent to make the deal go through.

The arrangement worked and soon both the office and

the site were buzzing with activity. The excavations were on in full swing. The customer centre, with its model apartment, miniature model of the community, renderings of the various views, sound and light show, and young nubile salesgirls and handsome salesboys, all trained and in snazzy attires, was put on priority and was nearing completion; it looked as good as the lobby of any premium luxury hotel in the world. There were consultations with priests, marketing agencies, PR agencies and several senior brokers in Noida to decide upon a good day and date to formally launch the sale of the first apartments in this future community.

As the day and date of the launch drew nearer, there were hectic parleys on which blocks would be sold first, the price structure, the floor rise pricing, the broker commissions, the upfront payments to be made by customers, and the agreement to be signed by them, which was a cleverly worded agreement to sale that only committed that they had the first right to the purchase of the apartment located in such-and-such building, on such-and-such floor. The financing companies and banks also wanted their clauses incorporated, and it took numerous meetings with lawyers and many sleepless nights to stitch the various pieces together.

Arun had absorbed it all; he was learning a lot, but there was a nagging sense of guilt at being a party to what was beginning to look like a scam. There were 1,200 apartments, and with each apartment potentially selling for close to a crore, the project would garner ₹1,200 crore for the Guptas, with an investment of only ₹3 crore. Such multiples made no sense to Arun, but he had not had the opportunity to chat with Sunil again on this. He promised himself that he would raise the issue and clear his doubts as he was becoming increasingly uncomfortable in this environment.

The big day dawned; there was much celebration and pomp at the puja conducted that morning. The cocktails and dinner that evening were a great success. They had set up a stall at the venue to record interest and bookings from potential customers; the lines there told the story of how successful the launch had been. Guptaji was beaming from ear to ear, and the Punk was busy trying to get some of the girls there to join him for an evening out after the formal event had ended.

As for Arun, he managed to track down Sunil Mathur. 'I can't understand the payment structure. We are charging a 10 per cent booking fee and giving 50 per cent of that back to the brokers. Is this how it works? If so, then for every apartment booked, the broker is making a cool ₹5 lakh; and we have received over seven hundred bookings today! The collection from the bookings is over ₹70 crore, which is far higher than what we have spent on this project till date,' Arun rattled off the facts.

Sunil was in an expansive mood. A single malt in his hand, he decided that Arun should learn all the facts. 'This is the Dickens of the real estate industry. Greed Expectations, my boy. Now, do you realize why everyone and their uncle wants to be a party to this? And you do not know half the story.' He leant in close to Arun and whispered, 'You are forgetting the cash collection of ₹10 lakh per apartment that that customer has to deposit with Guptaji's munim tomorrow morning. This is how this industry works, my friend. Have I told you what Mr Gupta plans to do with the money he has collected?'

Just as he was about to spill the beans, however, the Punk came looking for Arun and dragged him off to have a celebratory drink together.

The following morning, the appearance of the Rolls Royce Phantom had completed the picture for Arun. As he sat in the expensive car, he made a resolve. He would have nothing to do with this conniving, manipulative and exploitative and self-gratification culture. His belief in integrity, customer focus and reasonable returns had no place in this environment. He realized that he would end up a moral wreck if he continued to be a party to this game.

Changing Paradigms And Strategic Shifts

The bomb exploded with a finality that shook them into silence. Janus Designs, the company that Janaky Nathan and Nazreen Khan had formed eighteen months ago, was on the brink of downing shutters. The two of them, good friends through school and classmates at the National Institute of Fashion Technology (NIFT), had decided about two years ago to pool their skills and create a one-of-a-kind of business targeted at the aspiring Indian upper-middle class, and leverage the Indian diaspora around the world to give their company the global positioning and fillip it needed.

The road to the launch had not been easy. It began with the need for capital, and the constant rounds of visits to angel investors and funds, the routine presentations, the haggling and negotiations, the demands for an arm and a leg by the investors, and the long and dejected trundle back home. They had both lived through those depressing times and had often ended their days at their favourite watering hole with a bottle of wine between them, after which they would return to their shared apartment in the swank neighbourhood of Bandra with a resolve to attack the problem afresh the next morning.

Fortunately for them, about six months on, Janaky's cousin Amar, who was settled in the US, had come calling. Over a dinner, he had expressed a desire to bankroll them after hearing about their business strategy and plans, and on seeing the obvious passion both of them had for their Janus dream. Amar's only caveat was that he wanted them to keep their eyes on the goal of becoming cash positive by the end of the first year, and ensure that the venture stayed true to its vision of becoming a global brand with clear Indian leanings.

The investment of US $400,000 from Amar, coupled with their own seed capital of about US $100,000, had set the ship afloat in the high seas of the fashion business.

The next few months were a whirlwind of activity as they identified and finalized office space, vendors, material suppliers, artisans, distribution partners, bankers, event managers, PR personnel, and anything else that was needed to get the business off the ground. Janaky was the driver up front, playing the CEO to the hilt, serenading the distributors and wooing the exclusive outlets, influential magazines and the party animals on page three. Nazreen was the creative and constructive brains behind it all, the chief designer and head of operations, managing the concept sketches, design details, production and samples, costing and other details, trying to get the economics to work so they could inch closer to revenues and break even.

They both worked long hours; almost twenty hours each day, and more so on the weekends. Visits to exclusive outlets, cocktail parties, designer events and private shows were all part and parcel of their regime. All this led to both of them becoming increasingly dependent on alcohol to sustain their pace and energy levels. Janaky more so, as she was often the public face of their company, and it seemed that the industry thrived on a staple diet of vodka, martinis and cocktails.

Nazreen worried about it, though she herself was not far behind. She was aware that Janaky was the brains behind the marketing, pricing and visible brilliance, while she held the ship together with her iconic designs, her aesthetic sense, her ability to pick colour trends, and find the artisans to stitch it all together. Their lifestyle had become a whirlwind, and she knew they should be seriously worried about burning themselves out.

Then came demonetization, and all hell broke loose. Suddenly, 90 per cent of their sales disappeared as 90 per cent of their transactions were in cash; the Page 3 gangs did not believe in cheques and credit cards, and the starlets were used to being pampered by well-to-do businessmen who would rather leave no trails. Janaky and Nazreen had built their entire business model on the premise that they would keep their range exclusive and sought after and deal only with elite showrooms, which in turn catered to the top half per cent of the Indian population in the top three metros. It had seemed that the strategy was paying off, though of late they had serious doubts about the same as their debtors were standing at eight months worth of sales, after their distribution model was largely inclined towards a consignment basis sale, wherein retailers only paid for what they sold, over a period of time.

The stocks were returned by outlets; sales had to be reversed, some stocks were written off as sales were minimal at outlets. Their largest seller, Mehernaazs, made it clear that they would no longer stock or sell any of their products, as they would prefer to deal with known labels only going forward. Suddenly, the business was at a standstill. Costs kept rising and with no revenues, the dream start had turned into a nightmare.

Their CA, Mr Parekh, had visited them that morning and had told them, 'You have cash enough to survive for only two months; you can pay salaries to staff, rent and overheads, but you don't have enough to pay yourselves. Your financials for this financial year will show a loss of US $200,000, and the capital is all but eroded. I suggest you wind up the business, and both of you look for jobs.'

Janaky and Nazreen had both looked at each other, shell-shocked by the explosion so politely delivered by Mr Parekh. Mr Parekh was an old family friend of Janaky's father, and hence treated both of them like children, with kids gloves, yet with a finality of an order, on all that he said to them. They both walked slowly out of the office into the hot and humid Mumbai weather and made a beeline for their favourite watering hole, The Beaten Path. They couldn't help but remark on the irony of the name. They were truly beaten.

A few drinks down the hatch, and they both got their voices back.

'What do we do now? We are not going to work for someone else,' Nazreen empathically stated.

Janaky went further, 'We will turn this around and make Mr Parekh eat crow!'

Dutch courage reared its head. Soon realism countered, 'We need to speak with someone who understands how to run a business. We need to figure out if we can make our company survive and grow. Our inexperience has done us in.'

They both nodded in unison.

'Let me talk to Amar, we owe it to him,' Janaky continued.

She called him from the bar itself, and in a broken voice, told him the gist of what had happened. Amar heard them out but ended the conversation by saying, 'Let me talk to Malini about this.'

Neither knew what he meant.

The next day dawned, and they woke up nursing massive hangovers. They only had a vague recollection of the night before. Thanks to Uber, they had made it to their doorstep by themselves. When Janaky checked her mobile, she saw an email from Amar, addressed to Malini and copied to both of them. They picked up their mugs of coffee and read the email. It explained to Malini that Amar was mentoring and hand-holding Janus Designs and summed up their journey to date and the current situation.

Malini Mehta came with impressive credentials. An MBA from IIM Bangalore, a stint at Mckinsey & Co, where she grew to a partner, then started her own boutique consulting business. She was regarded as one of the best brains in strategy in the S&MEs space. She was in fact a keynote speaker on all forums where SMEs were mentioned, while serving on the boards of several blue-chip organizations in the country.

She was Amar's classmate from school, and Amar had reached out to her. Ten minutes later, Janaky's phone rang.

'Hi, this is Malini. I just read Amar's mail and was wondering if I could meet the two of you today?'

To the point, no nonsense, with a strong bias for action, Janaky concluded. After agreeing to meet that afternoon, Janaky and Nazreen got to work getting their hangovers out of their systems with a workout and a shower, and a good breakfast to top it off.

They met Malini for lunch and after getting the pleasantries out of the way, got down to business. Nazreen and Janaky filled Malini in on the business: their revenue model, their cost structures, their pricing strategy, their vision of becoming a global brand with a local twist, their journey so far, their business growth and development strategies, their brush with demonetization and the subsequent unravelling of everything and the company's current precarious position. They minced no words nor did they offer any excuses. Malini heard them out patiently, asked a few follow-up questions and then sought an afternoon to think through everything she had learnt before getting back to them.

As promised, the following morning there was a detailed email from Malini waiting for them in their inboxes. She had outlined a few action points for them to execute immediately. They ran something like this:

- Go back to square one. Do a blue sky think again.
- Revisit your positioning strategy for the product.
- Rework your pricing accordingly. Redo the distribution strategy.
- Shift the marketing focus to alternative media.
- Increase the point of sale and viral networks.
- Recast the business plan and make sure exigency funds are provided for.

She concluded her mail, by saying that once they had done all that she had suggested, they should meet again.

Janaky and Nazreen got busy with acting on Malini's suggestions. But try as they might, they could not get beyond the first one. Their rethink kept bringing them back to their current approach and soon led to raised voices, defensive stances and running around in circles.

That's when Janaky decided that they would have to talk to Malini and try and think things through together. Malini graciously agreed to meet them, perhaps sensing the unspoken despair and cry for help in Janaky's voice.

Malini kicked off the meeting with, 'Let me walk you through the thinking and reasons behind what I stated in my email.

'I find that your strategy assumes that you will be welcomed with open arms, as an established designer label would. It's a crowded and very competitive space and making inroads by going head-on is difficult and not a very good strategic move.

'Positioning yourselves against established designers is not viable as the price premium that entails is not what your customer will be willing to pay. Redefine your customer. Your base cannot be the glitterati and Bollywood who's who right off the bat.'

They both nodded in agreement.

Malini continued. 'If your customer is the upper-middle class and affluent, socially active woman within the age group of twenty to forty-five years, then think about where she lives and socializes. The three major metros are a very small percentage of the population. You need to go into more cities.'

Janaky and Nazreen agreed on the customer profile and Malini went on.

'Your pricing needs to reflect the segment you are catering to, as do your distribution points. Mehernaazs is not the ideal retail outlet for you. Target outlets that cater to the segment in Pune, Hyderabad, Ahmedabad, Kolkata, Chandigarh, Lucknow, Bhopal, Coimbatore, Chennai and the likes.

'Also, no selling on a consignment basis. That is a guaranteed formula for retail lethargy. There will be no interest in promoting the product. I recommend that you price yourselves more aggressively and offer a prompt payment discount and collect the outstanding.

'The pricing strategy should position the product for the target audience. The range should be between ₹25,000 and ₹200,000 for the upper end of the spectrum. That price point is comfortably placed to be an attractive proposition for all the upwardly mobile, social ladies.

'Your customers are also technology savvy. So, a clear online model of review and purchase is an essential part of the strategy. The online-offline model is a must as part of distribution in this segment.

'Digital payments are also a must. Credit cards, e-wallets and net banking must be part of your offering and options. Move all marketing efforts to the digital and online spaces. It is much more cost-effective and easier to execute.

'Leverage your own social circles, your Linkedin, Facebook and Whatsapp lists, to get your friends and acquaintances to talk about and actively explore and purchase your designs.

'Hold a garage sale of all the inventory that has come back to you. Offer special deals to upwardly mobile professionals who would love to be seen in your designs. This will help liquidate the stocks and convert them into cash, a scarce commodity for you today.

'And finally, shift the focus of your below-the-line activities to tier-two towns and cities. Move the emphasis to professional enclaves and high-end residential gated communities to build awareness and trial.'

All that she had expounded made sense to both Nazreen and Janaky. They got down to business the very next day. The business model was recast, the pricing reset, the marketing initiatives moved to digital and the website redesign was commissioned on a priority basis. Net banking, payment gateways and credit card facilities were set up. Janaky then set off on a long tour to get the distribution expansion initiative going.

The results were far beyond their wildest expectations. Nazreen's designs were a hit online, the demand outstripped supply by miles, retailers were willing to pay upfront for stocks, inventory was down to ten days' stocks, online orders started coming in from overseas as well, and Janaky had to do a whirlwind tour of the key diaspora markets to sign up partners for expansion to those shores. Janus Designs had arrived with a bang.

They had broken even and were now rolling in cash. Amar proposed that he and his friends invest US $2 million to fund the next stage of growth. They had, in the spirit of sharing, announced an employee stock option plan for their core team, which had worked crazy hours to ensure the plan was executed and to meet the demands of a rapidly growing order book.

As they sat celebrating their success with their core team, and the champagne, at the coolest hangout in town, both Nazreen and Janaky, made a mental note to pay a visit to Malini, and pay their dues to what could only be termed as a divine intervention. Every thought of hers had translated into huge gains for them, and they both wanted to sign her up as an advisor for a long time to come.

Reality Aftershocks

Kaustubh Khopikar, an idealist since his schooldays, was in a heated argument with his co-founders, K. Sundaresan and Atul Malhotra. All three of them were erstwhile senior banking executives and had come together about three years ago with a dream of creating a financial institution focused on the impact sector. The growing yet underfunded S&MEs sector was classically underserved for debt, as was evident from innumerable studies and reports published by both government and private agencies. Indeed, the sector had also been neglected by the bank they had formerly worked at, a leading multinational that was amongst the top four banks globally. It was this that had prompted them to call it quits and try to set up a NBFC that would address exactly this gap.

Their idealism, passion and desire to genuinely contribute to Indian society had brought them together, and they had diligently attacked the task of setting up exactly that. They had been fortunate enough to interest the Global Development Fund in their project, thanks to the connect that Kaustubh had with the global head for emerging markets for the Fund, Ashwin Jain. Ashwin had been Kaustubh's first boss and had liked the idea and the team of co-founders. Thanks to his support and active lobbying, the GDF had agreed to bankroll the company with a hefty initial investment of US$ 50 million.

They had identified the areas of competence and experience that each of them brought to the table, and had played their respective roles to the hilt; Sundaresan had donned the hat of the COO, Kaustubh the CEO and Atul the CFO. Several employees from the bank they had previously worked at, had also reached out to them, and they had hired a few for other critical roles as well. The strategy and planning for the business was entrusted to a multinational consulting firm, and they had put together the market mapping and identified opportunities, the financial model, the process maps, the structure, the controls and checks, the roadmap for expansion, the product ideas, and the sourcing and collections procedures. In their wisdom, they had recommended that every function be in-house, which gelled with the bankers and their old boys' club.

A quick acquisition of a shell company with the requisite licences had given them the necessary fillip, and they could proudly present to their Board the fact that they were ahead of plan on the implementation, six months down the road. The first few quarters were hunky-dory. Roll-out was happening, training was in full swing, bankers and partners were crowding their offices, and their swank corporate office in the financial district was inaugurated with much fanfare. Smug and confident, the team had started the practice of celebrations on a weekly basis, to let the world and their employees know of their success.

The end of the financial year saw them report numbers that stood the test of benchmarking versus plan, though in terms of expansion of branches, they had fallen behind. The Board had sounded them off, with Kaustubh being specifically instructed to reach out to fellow NBFCs and seek comparative performance numbers to ratify the assumptions and ratios as projected. The environment had started to spiral downwards, and the ripples of global upheavals began to be felt in the Indian market as well. The financial services space in particular bore the brunt of the cascading effect of the collapse of two global financial institutions. However, their company, Fortune Financial Services, Kaustubh was quick to point out, had managed to maintain its key performance indicators within acceptable levels and ranges. Atul reiterated that their cash flows were looking good, and they had managed to procure a line of credit in excess of US $150 million from a consortium of banks. In fact, they now needed to call in the next round of equity investment committed by the Fund.

Then came the first signs of cracks in the ceiling. The first two quarters of the next financial year saw operating costs shooting up, delinquencies beginning to slip, asset accretion slowing, corporate overheads seeing the full impact of the new office and fresh hires, financial costs rising and a blame-game culture seeping in. The snowballing of all of this resulted in the numbers being missed by a mile, and the half-yearly Board review was disastrous for all three of them. They had taken the brunt of it, but the differences among them regarding the reasons for the debacle had surfaced in the meeting. They had been pushed to the wall, and their self-protection instincts, honed in the multinational environment of their erstwhile employer, had kicked in.

They walked away, each one looking for a scapegoat who could take the fall and thus, to give them the time they needed to pull up their socks and get the business back on track. A senior business head was the first to go; he was the weakest link in the old boys' club as he had come from a subsidiary of the bank, and there was no history of rum and coke sessions worth talking about in the past. This sent panic signals down the line, and the human resources team was inundated with calls from insecure employees and counselling sessions became a common sight in the corporate office. Attrition started rearing its head. Several field and mid-level executives decided to seek employment elsewhere. Gaps in key functions meant loss of operational efficiencies, further aggravating the situation.

The trend had only gotten worse. The second financial year performance was an unmitigated disaster. The Board had announced the beginning of the countdown; one more fiscal disaster year, and the entire leadership team would have to start looking for other options.

Sundaresan, Kaustubh and Atul, who till then had been playing the who-blinks-first game, decided to put their differences behind them, and a keen collective survival instinct took over.

'We need to do something drastic. We do not have a choice,' was how Kaustubh had voiced it, and that had started the present argument.

'Who is responsible for this situation?' Sundaresan countered.

To which Atul responded, 'Operating costs and overheads!'

Sundaresan turned to him with, 'Who is responsible for managing our finance costs and budgets? Why are we way out of whack?'

Kaustubh decided to bring the argument to a close.

'Let's not debate who, but focus on the what, and how to

fix it. Kartik Ramanathan, who has spent years in the NBFC space, is a very dear friend. He is considered to be the father of the NBFC business in India. I am going to ask him to spend a day with us, go through our numbers and give us his unbiased opinion on what could be wrong and how we can fix it.'

Both Atul and Sundaresan had heard of Kartik and had to accept that this was one business that he possibly knew better than all of them put together. So, reluctantly, they agreed to meet Rajesh as soon as possible. All their travel and other plans could wait. There could be nothing more critical, they unanimously agreed.

The four of them met the following Saturday in the boardroom of the corporate office. Barring a few housekeeping staff, they had made sure no one else was aware of the meeting with Kartik. Kaustubh set the ball rolling, presenting the key metrics, their history over the past few years, the current data and their key areas of concern. Kartik heard him out patiently and then asked the three of them a few questions, all the while making notes and jotting down data points.

'Where are we going wrong, and what are we missing, Kartik?' Kaustubh asked.

Kartik began by saying, 'What I am going to tell you may not be very palatable as I am going to tell it as it is. It is up to the three of you to decide the merit of what I share and take the necessary action to address the issues. My observations may seem random, but they are all linked to the way you have gone about the business. I suggest you take notes; they will come in handy.'

Then began their education. They learnt that executing an operating plan for an NBFC required a different mindset and entailed new learnings and practices. The standards and benchmarks in the sector were different from those in banking, the people and processes were different from what they knew, and the monitoring and control interventions were of a very different order.

Kartik made several points. 'Your cost structures are out of control; your corporate overheads and operating and branch costs are unviable. With the corporate overheads at this level, you need an asset book of ₹30,000 crore to cover for them. You should cut the corporate overheads to 20 per cent of what they are today.

'For a 2000-employee organization you have five hundred people in the head office. You don't need more than a hundred. You are not running an MNC bank country office. Even that doesn't have so many employees in the head office.

'Your operating cost per account is as high as ₹10,000 per account. At that level, your interest income from each account has to be at least ₹36, 000 per year, assuming no losses and no overheads. At an average ticket size of one lakh, that's never going to happen.

'Your branch offices are 1,500 square feet, air-conditioned spaces with ten employees per branch. You will need a portfolio of at least ₹50 crore per branch to cover branch costs. At 1 lakh rupee loans, you will require at least 5,000 customers per branch, which doesn't look viable. Cut them down to 25 per cent of this cost, to make any sense for the business.

'Your organizational structure is not sustainable. You have credit risk reporting to the individual business verticals. This will result in spiralling losses and frauds. Keep them balanced as they need to counterbalance each other. Have a matrix structure if need be.

'Why are all your operations centralized and sitting in

prime real estate? Why is everything in-house? By outsourcing it, moving some of the functions to the outskirts, you can cut your per account cost to less than half of what it is.

'Technology should enable efficiencies for the business. Figure out if you can move it to a less capital-intensive model. It's very expensive the way it is'.

'You are also very top heavy as an organization. You have too many expensive resources, which an NBFC cannot sustain. This is not banking, where that can be supported.

'You also have too many resources in your support functions. The ratio of line to staff function employees is 1:4. It should be 1:15 or so. Your productivity targets for the branches are too loose. Move them significantly higher.

'And finally, you don't need IIM MBA graduates at all levels of the organization. Graduates from colleges should also do. Don't overdesign everything; it will lead to frustrations and attritions later. You cannot afford it.'

Kaustubh, Sundaresan and Atul had to swallow their pride and accept that what Kartik had said made sense. He had also given them data on benchmarks with other NBFCs to endorse what he had said. They looked at each other and exchanged a silent acceptance of their mistakes, and a vow to act immediately! Humbled and with their egos shattered, they trooped out of the room, but with every step, their shoulders straightened a little, their eyes began to light up and their confidence started to return; they knew they had a chance at fixing things. Their vision of creating something they could be proud of was still intact and seemed more achievable now.

No Free Lunches

It all began eight years ago. Prabhakar Kale had returned from the US with a postgraduate degree under his belt and a reasonable stint in the specialized steel sector. He had visions of creating what his idol, Mr Mittal, had created in the steel industry. His vision had been to establish a special steel unit that could cater to the advanced steel requirements of the defence, components and pumps and associated devices in the stainless steel sector. He had enthusiastically put together his business plan, gathered his savings and sent a techno-feasibility report to a few leading and small banks for a project financing proposal. He had been introduced to Process Design House, a Nagpur-based company headquartered not far from his own sprawling bungalow, which had done all the design and grunt work for a hefty fee and was committed to helping him set up the plant once the loan was approved.

He, in all his earnestness, had started engaging with

potential buyers and suppliers and had joined several relevant associations and local bodies as well as the Rotary International Club in Nagpur, with a view to furthering his network of acquaintances and associates. It was at an event hosted by one of these associations that he was introduced to Mr Fernandez, a senior banker in one of the established private banks, and had crossed paths with Mr Bhushan, a small-time steel manufacturer. He soon became good friends with both and they would often drop in at Prabhakar's bungalow for a drink-and-dinner session. However, the two were never at Prabhakar's house together, as Bhushan and Fernandez did not really know each other. Prabhakar thought himself blessed for having such knowledgeable and well-connected friends.

Things had moved along nicely. The loan had been approved and the construction of the factory commenced. Visits to potential customers showed promising signs of long-term contracts. Steel raw material prices stayed well within the realms of his production costing assumptions. The only thing that Prabhakar was not happy about, though it had to be done, was that he had had to mortgage his bungalow to the bank as part of the collateral required for the banking lines and the working capital support. It still bothered him at night as he lay sleepless with excitement and anticipation at the thought of the commencement of production and his first orders; it was the only blemish in an otherwise rosy picture.

His business got off to a good start; the first orders were from Bhushan's factory, albeit a sub-contract for supply to a leading large steel mill. The margins were small, but the promise of a never-ending order book made Prabhakar compromise on critical parameters in the contract. The pricing was low, the credit terms were easy, the delivery schedules were tight with penalties for delayed deliveries, the knowhow transfer was a five-year, close-ended clause, and Prabhakar had agreed to all of it for Bhushan's sake. He had felt a sense of obligation to both Bhushan and Fernandez and had tied himself to steep costs, adverse conditions and severe penalties and restrictions with both the buyer and the bank. The financial year had ended with a small operating loss, though with the finance costs of the bank, it meant that he had had to dig deep into his savings to fund the gap.

Then began the meltdown. The steel industry went into in turmoil thanks to cheaper Chinese steel products and the resulting downward spiral cycle for the industry yanked the carpet from under the feet of Prabhakar's company. The demand curve went south; Prabhakar's buyers cut back on their orders, renegotiated prices and switched to imported Chinese components, thus pushing his company to the wall. The only saving grace was Bhushan's company, which continued to buy, but with revised purchase prices, which squeezed his margins to wafer thin. On the other hand, the global financial meltdown had made the banks revisit their terms, and his finance costs went up by over 200 basis points. All this led to significant losses and his company, Specialised Steel Products, was on the verge of eating completely into its capital.

Today, Prabhakar was sitting opposite Fernandez to seek an increase in the credit limits and more time to pay the overdue finance charges, as the company had defaulted on them.

'I cannot help you on this, Prabhakar,' Fernandez said with a note of finality. 'Though we understand the downturn and the steel sector crisis, we lent you money based on your ability to make good the interest costs and the principal on time. You are already behind on your payments and I will need the arrears to be cleared immediately. Else we will be forced to close the loan and seek alternative means of recovery. Your bungalow, which is mortgaged to us, is worth at least twice what you owe us; I am sure you wouldn't want to lose that,' was his ominous warning.

A sad and forlorn Prabhakar returned to his office only to find Bhushan waiting to see him. 'Prabhakar, we have to talk!' Prabhakar ushered Bhushan into his office, closed the door and then began the second uncomfortable conversation of the day.

'You have missed your delivery schedules, and hence I have to invoke the penalty clause. I hope you appreciate that this is only business. Our friendship shall remain intact,' Bhushan added to soften the blow.

It was a lethal body blow. The clause stipulated a discount of 5 per cent on the price per week of delay, and they were already two weeks behind. A quick mental calculation told Prabhakar he would end up making a loss of 5 per cent on the transaction overall, given the delayed delivery schedule. Bhushan soon left, smug in the knowledge that he had made a killing on the price revision.

That night Prabhakar had yet another difficult conversation, this time with his wife. 'I will need to find at least ₹15 crore of capital immediately. Otherwise, I will have to shut down the business and give up this bungalow. Between Fernandez and Bhushan, I need to make good that much. Raghav has also endorsed the need.'

Raghav was Prabhakar's CA and had helped him put his books in order for the past five years.

'Where will you get the money from? The private equity infusion you have been pursuing for so long has been a dead end. Neither have your friends come forward to help,' Ragini echoed his thoughts.

Prabhakar sat quietly for a while, and then said, 'Raghav says he knows someone who can lend us the money, but the catch is the source of the money is dubious, and a large part of it will come in cash. I am now thinking of exploring that option.'

'Why are you even thinking of doing such a thing? Don't we have enough problems already? The kind of people that Raghav seems to be recommending are not the type either you or I can deal with.'

Prabhakar knew that Ragini made sense, but he could not see any other way of getting out of this conundrum.

'I do not have a choice, my dear. I will have to explore this option, thoroughly and quickly.' With that, Prabhakar picked up the phone and dialled Raghav to ask him to set up a meeting with the potential investors at the earliest.

The meeting was a very strange one. It was held in a farmhouse on the outskirts of Mumbai. He and Raghav flew down, and the meeting lasted a full six hours. The gist was that he had to agree to a stake of 51 per cent for the investing party for an investment of ₹20 crore. Mr Gavande, the lawyer and representative of the investor, had also insisted that they accept ₹8 crore of the investment in cash. Hence Prabhakar had to agree to part with 51 per cent of his company for ₹12 crore, and the paperwork was to be drawn up accordingly. The cash would come without any record of that part of the transaction. It was a terribly one-sided bargain, having to sell his company that had a net worth of at least ₹30 crore at this garage-sale price. They agreed to meet two weeks later to sign the final documentation, and the money would then be transferred to Prabhakar and Ragini's accounts.

The day for the signing dawned. Prabhakar flew to Mumbai

to ink the deal that would hopefully help him get out of the mess he had gotten into. There was obviously the new complication of the unknown investor, and the fact that he had to give away 51 per cent of his company. The only thing his lawyer had ensured was that the management of the company would remain in Prabhakar's hands. As he waited in the coffee shop of the Trident Hotel, Prabhakar was shocked to see Bhushan walk in. *I do not need this*, he was thinking to himself, when in walked Fernandez as well. They both came forward with wide grins on their faces; and following them was a gentleman who looked very familiar to Bhushan.

'Hi, Prabhakar. This is Ranjan, my elder brother, who is your investor,' Bhushan said, clearing the air.

'I am his banker,' Fernandez chipped in.

Prabhakar was aghast. It dawned on him that the whole series of incidents had in fact been a carefully engineered plan. Now he was well and truly enmeshed in their scheme and he saw his company slipping out of his hands, slowly but surely. All his efforts, education and struggles had come to naught thanks to the two wily gentlemen who were now sitting opposite him and grinning gleefully, enjoying his discomfort and obvious pain. The deed was done, and he now had to drive the final nail into his own coffin, Prabhakar realized. It also meant that the two gentlemen were privy to all the nuances of the transactions, and he would be forced to settle their claims on a priority basis.

A week later, Prabhakar had a very different kind of a meeting with both Fernandez and Bhushan. The tone, manner and discussions were exactly the opposite of the grief they had earlier given him.

'Now that we are dealing with my brother's company, I am willing to waive the penalty clause. So we can go back to our earlier terms. I am also increasing the order to three times the size, now that I know you can fund the inventory and work in process,' Bhushan generously offered.

'The bank will also increase your working capital line to 15 crore, and the interest costs will now be only 12 per cent as against the earlier 15.5 per cent, given that Mr Ranjan is a very important and valued customer for us,' Fernandez declared with a smile.

'There is just one thing you need to do for us before that happens,' they both said in unison, after a brief break when their drinks had arrived.

'Now what?' asked Prabhakar, dispensing with the need to be formal with them as he now regarded both of them as conniving creeps.

'We need some cash; about ₹1 crore each. This will ensure we stay grounded and treat you well going forward. So, let's meet again tomorrow, here at the club, and get us the money in plastic carry bags to avoid suspicion. It is great to have a friend like you!'

With these parting words, both Bhushan and Fernandez left him holding the bill for the evening and with grave misgivings for the road ahead.

He kept castigating himself for having so foolishly fallen for the game. It also dawned on him that Raghav needed to go; none of this could have happened without his knowledge and tacit concurrence. He remembered Ragini's warning when she had asked him to get a professional opinion from a reputed chartered accounting and consulting firm before signing away his company to Ranjan, who was a new animal he had to deal with. She had even dissuaded him from agreeing to the cash component, which was risk-prone, and could sully their reputation in society at large.

But then desperation had prevailed. It was too late; he now had to salvage what he could from the business, and the fact that he had an order book and a bank line that could both help him turn the corner was small consolation. He got up and headed back to his office, promising himself that he would never again take the easy way out. There clearly was karmic justice in life.

The Perils Of Legacy

V. Subaraman had taken over as the head of manufacturing and operations of the subsidiary of the boutique manufacturing company, Higrid Tools, a European company specializing in cutting tools and fixtures catering to special usages from drills to cutting, milling and CNC machines across a wide variety of sectors. Higrid Tools had acquired Parekh Tools about three years ago, and they were still in the process of integrating the same into their global operations. The headquarters of the Indian company, which was in a small town in Gujarat, was one of the legacies they were dealing with amongst the many challenges that were facing them. Subaraman's brief was to try and make the business self-sustaining in terms of contribution margins, and subsequently develop India as a hub for the company's global manufacturing.

During the eighteen months he had spent at the headquarters, he had given it all he had. He had used his experience, his quality certifications, his engineering mind, his undivided attention and efforts, his people handling skills to make the manufacturing set-up viable, in the fond hope that he would then be given a role in the global manufacturing team, an ambition he secretly nurtured. But all his efforts seemed to come to naught; the financials as reported by the CFO, Shahid Wani, indicated that the proposition continued to bleed, and the Board was now seriously contemplating selling the Indian arm of the business. Suba had discussed the issue with some of his friends, and one of them had suggested appointing a seasoned consultant to look at the business in totality and recommend strategic steps to turn it around.

The CEO of the Indian operation, Robert Mortimer, a citizen of the UK, had recently taken over and agreed with Subaraman's suggestion of an independent evaluation of the business. They had both come to Mumbai to meet the professional who had been strongly recommended by several of Suba's acquaintances and friends who had experience in such matters. As they waited for Mr Haridas Pai, the consultant, in the lobby of the JW Marriot, they discussed the brief that they should give him. There were certain aspects of the business that tended to further complicate matters. The four different manufacturing units, separated by a few hundred metres within one industrial pocket, the legacy machines and systems, which were barely used but formed part of the purchase, the strained labour equations, which were slowly coming under control but still posed product quality challenges, were just a few of these troublesome factors.

Mr Pai walked in at precisely 11.00 a.m. as agreed, which Suba and Bob were quick to notice and thought it augured well. After a brief round of introductions and the establishing of common friends among them, they got down to business. Bob briefly summed up the company's current business reality, including the fact that it was still in the red, and Suba added the manufacturing challenges and the legacy issues they were contending with.

Pai heard them out and then asked, 'Is there a brief for me to address? The problem is fairly large, and if all of it is to be within the scope of the assessment, it would take a good year or two to identify, address and resolve. I would also like to see the financials and some basic data to help me understand the problem better.'

Suba and Bob invited him to their Mumbai office, where their CFO, Mr Shahid Wani, sat. They decided to meet there the next morning.

Pai, Suba, Bob and Shahid met in the Mumbai liaison office, located in Andheri East. A small office, consisting largely of the accounts and finance team, with a few cabins for visiting executives and Bob, it seemed to be another legacy from the past. Pai was surprised to see no sales and marketing personnel based there, but refrained from commenting. Shahid did all the talking.

'We acquired this company, Parekh Tools, in 2010, lock, stock and barrel. The four factories, this office and my team and I were inherited from Parekh. I stayed on as the CFO at the request of the global chairman and Board, and have been operating from here since. We inherited accumulated losses and some inventory along with a set of clients, who we still service and deal with. The contribution margin of the business is very poor, and I have not been able to get Bob here to move the prices up to get us out of the red. His claim is that we are inefficient, but Suba here refutes that.'

Suba and Bob exchanged glances, which Pai noticed.

Shahid continued after a brief pause as tea arrived for all of them. 'We have revenues of US $6 million, exports of about US $2 million, but have been making a loss of about US $800,000 for the past few years. The accumulated losses today stand at about US $2 million, and the Board and I are concerned as to whether this business will ever see the light at the end of the tunnel.'

Pai asked a few questions on the fixed overheads, labour costs and cost of factory operations, and Shahid promised that his associate, Ms Nutan, would provide the answers and data by the end of the day. Shahid further added, 'I think the issue is the four separate manufacturing set-ups, which lead to inefficiencies of overheads, incidentals and labour, amongst other things.'

Pai wanted to visit the factories in order to understand this better, and Suba agreed to coordinate the visit. After the meeting, the mandate given to Mr Pai was to conduct the factory assessments and opportunities to improve efficiencies while consolidating, to begin with, which he would present to the global CEO and chairman when they were in India for the Board meeting in December, about three months away.

The day of reckoning dawned. Suba had been invited to attend the Board meeting as a special invitee as the agenda was largely centred on Mr Pai's findings and recommendations. He was nervous; he had no idea what Pai would throw up, and he had seen enough of him to know that he would not mince words. The meeting commenced, and Mr Pai rose and addressed the group. After a brief outline of his profile, previous experience, mandate and his methodology, he began to present his findings.

'The business runs on a contribution margin of 55 per cent. Hence, there is no reason why the same should not translate into a profit before tax of at least 30 per cent. This is based on data provided by your finance and Management Information Systems teams.

'Your fixed corporate overheads are to the tune of US $2.3 million, largely the cost of the executives in the room. In line with this, your bottom line should be at least US $1.2 million every year.'

Shahid immediately jumped in, 'Examining the financials was not part of your brief. You were to only evaluate the factories and synergies, if any.'

The chairman of the Board, Mr Johanssen, however, brushed Shahid's concern aside. 'Please go ahead, Mr Pai. We would like to know more.'

Pai continued. 'The manufacturing and direct cost inefficiencies, due to the split manufacturing units, are only to the tune of US $200,000. Eliminating that will only add marginally to the bottom line. All data are presented in the three annexures of your copy of the report.

'The cost of manufacture, in reality, is only 25 per cent; the rest is comprised of amortization of the acquisition cost, depreciation and the cost of executives like Suba, who are based out of the factory. There is an incorrect classification of costs, which presents a skewed picture.

'Some other interesting data points, which may bear investigating, are that the material losses in transit and manufacturing are running as high as 12 per cent, and inventory seems to be high at more than a year's worth of stock. Your corporate overheads need a serious relook; no manufacturing business can or should live with a number of 40 per cent.'

Johanssen interrupted him to ask, 'What is your hypothesis, Mr Pai? You have led large multinationals and are well-versed in our workings, methods and commitment to running an ethical business. What is the bottom line for us?'

'I think this is a 35 per cent EBITDA business, at least. I would refuse to accept anything else,' Pai responded. 'I would initiate a complete audit of the inventory, with a special focus on the losses in transit and manufacturing as well. And I would use India as the global manufacturing hub for the Southeast Asian and Western Asian markets, given its strategic cost and locational advantages,' Pai concluded.

Shahid stepped in and said dismissively, 'Okay. Your role is over. Suba will see you out.'

Johanssen intervened, 'Mr Pai, please join us for lunch; we are grateful to you for your efforts and succinct summary. We have some serious thinking to do.'

After a quick lunch and some polite social exchanges, Mr Pai excused himself and was politely escorted to the elevators by Mr Johanssen.

A few months later, Suba and Bob gave Pai a call.

'We would like to meet you for lunch tomorrow, at the Marriot in Mumbai. Please make yourself available. We have plenty to update you on.'

Pai agreed to meet them the following day at noon.

Bob started the conversation by saying, 'We are extremely grateful to you for your assessment and your findings. You saved both our jobs. We have not had the opportunity to thank you personally.'

Pai acknowledged the thanks and Bob continued. 'Mr Johanssen was very impressed with you. He immediately tasked Ernst & Young, our auditors, to conduct a forensic audit in the areas you outlined.

'Your suspicions were true. There was an artificial inflation of inventory, and inventory in transit was missing by the truckloads.

'We restated our books after taking an on-time hit in the past year. So, we are now a healthy, profitable subsidiary.

'Suba has been inducted on the Board and given the additional responsibility for quality assurance, globally.'

There was a pregnant pause. Pai had a distinct feeling that they were not telling him the full story. He looked at Suba and asked, 'So who was the fox in the hole? There had to be an insider who was orchestrating what was going on.'

Suba and Bob looked at each other and Bob smiled as he said, 'Shahid was found with his hand in the till; he has been arrested and put behind bars. He has paid the company US $5 million to withdraw the charges and seek a lower sentence.'

'He was making money and balancing the books by showing a higher physical inventory than what actually existed. He was also showing higher costs for the same quantity manufactured, to cover the in-transit pilferage, which he had orchestrated,' Suba added. 'Your summary to Johanssen pushed him to act on our suspicions. We shall remain eternally grateful to you for putting us back on track.'

Pai smiled and in parting, said, 'One of the challenges of an acquisition in India is the perils of the legacy that you inherit. More often than not, the rot is transferred to the buyer, unless you consciously conduct a surgery. Revisit all assumptions from a zero base whenever you do so.'

The two executives could only nod in acceptance, and mentally etch this sage advice in their minds for life!

Bootstrapping To a Fault

Divakar Pandey and Ankush Jha were hard at work, finetuning their business model as the final step towards launching their venture, ProcessBazaar, a concept aimed at bringing together outsourcing service providers and midsize corporates wishing to outsource for cost and operational efficiencies. The platform had been created with a lot of thought and sleepless nights and was based on their collective experience in their respective fields of financial services and healthcare. It offered a marketplace model for both sides to come together for a win-win through effective and efficient outsourcing. Their company, as the exchange, would derive its revenues from the nominal charge for registering on their site. The larger game plan was to leverage the databases thus created to cross and upsell ancillary services to both sides of the outsourcing model.

They had put their hard-earned savings into creating the product platform and ensuring the intellectual property remained protected; they had heard horror stories about what had happened to organizations that had failed to do so. This paranoia had also made them pull out all the stops with regard to the security set-up, and hence they had overshot their planned outlay for the same. Now, both Divakar and Ankush were scraping the bottom of the barrel to find the money to fund their drive to sign up potential suppliers of outsourcing services and clients for outsourcing as the first set of registered users. They had planned to go live with their offering the previous Monday, but had deferred it as the service lines for handling customer queries and calls were yet to be activated.

So near, yet so far, was the thought on both their minds. They had exhausted the last capital penny they had raised and would now have to approach their friends and family, who had largely funded their venture, to seek more funds to move ahead. But that was easier said than done. Their funders had started asking questions, some uncomfortable, some downright insulting, as to where the funds had disappeared. They both knew that the other two investors in the venture besides themselves could easily contribute another ₹5 lakh each; this, combined with the additional ₹10 lakh each that they themselves could put in would take them through the next 5 to 6 months at least. However, they were also wrestling with the decision of how much they should spend on launching the business.

Divakar believed that they should invest in building the team for business development as it was critical that they show immediate traction, and hence be in a better position to establish the proof of concept and thus be more attractive to the next set of early investors. Ankush had radically different views. Their differences had come to light during the previous evening's meeting with the investment advisor they had spoken to,

Mr Arun Verma. Arun had been referred to them by a common friend, who had had many complimentary things to say about Mr Verma. They had found that to be true; in fact, they had found that Arun's perspective, gained through years of experience, had added to their own understanding of the business.

The conversation last evening had stalled as Ankush had brought up the issue of office space. 'I don't think we need an office at this time; we should operate from a Starbucks, as we have been doing so far. I am also against hiring three people for the business development team as we cannot afford them right now; we should do whatever we can ourselves.'

Divakar had put forward his views. 'We need to invest in business development and in an office space as customers will see an office as proof that we are a serious concern. Moreover, we also need a customer service team to address complaints and queries and help in the creation of online masters. The bankers also need the same.'

Arun, who had been a witness to this tug of war, had gently chimed in. 'So, are you guys going to try and build this business as a two-member team? That would mean you will have to quit your regular jobs and work full-time on your venture from tomorrow.'

Neither of them had quit their respective jobs till then as they had envisaged a long period of slow growth given the nature of business. They had started on this journey while still employed and had successfully brought things to where they were today.

Again, there were two voices.

'I am quitting this Friday,' said Divakar.

Ankush, however, had been a little more circumspect. 'I will see how things go for a few months before I quit.'

'But then how will you get the work done without hiring anyone else? Building a business from scratch is more than a full-time job; it means long hours of passionate, dedicated and really hard work. Will your current job allow you to do that?' Arun had questioned.

'Aren't you defeating the purpose of this start-up by not providing the resources, teeth and energy it needs to succeed? You have spent ₹3.5 crore in researching and building a product and yet today you are talking about not spending ₹1.2 lakh a month for a business development team. This is like building a hotel and not spending on the resources to man and run it. Do not cut off your nose to spite your face,' had been Arun's warning.

The meeting had ended without a decision on what next steps they should take. Both Divakar and Ankush were left wondering what the right thing to do would be. Divakar was upset with Ankush for deciding not to put in his papers; they had agreed to do so together on the coming Friday. As they left the meeting, he decided to have a word with him.

'Ankush, we need to arm the team with hunters. We also need farmers to service and cream the accounts. Let's not cut corners on this,' he appealed.

'Where are we going to get the funding to support this from? We barely have enough to last us six months, without the team. Once we hire a team, we will exhaust our funds in two months. Let's make our money last,' was Ankush's rejoinder.

This chicken-and-egg debate went on for a while, but there was no end in sight. They both understood the need to resolve it and move ahead, but each was standing firm on his position. They had also committed to hiring office space in Gurgaon, which needed to be formalized soon.

Ultimately, they took the middle path. They went ahead and hired two business development personnel and one customer service resource all experienced individuals from established organizations who were seeking to be part of a start-up with significant opportunities for an upside. They formalized and moved into the office space they had identified. The move brought dynamism to the venture. The soft launch went off without a hitch, and the team members attacked the two ends of the spectrum, identifying organizations looking to outsource their activities and suppliers willing to execute these activities. They were making slow but steady progress. However, the sword of Damocles hanging over their heads gave both Divakar and Ankush sleepless nights, and things soon came to a boiling point.

It all started with the teams' salaries not being paid for a month, twice in a row. They were understandably bitter about it and wanted adequate assurances and dates by when they would be paid. Divakar and Ankush reassured them but could not give them the requested payment date. The three team members, in turn, went ahead and started seeking opportunities elsewhere, and within a span of two weeks, all three had found other jobs. Naturally, this impacted the business. Client issues began increasing. Not only that, potential clients on the verge of signing up started expressing concerns regarding the start-up's ability to last the course and began having second thoughts about signing up. The rent for the premises also got delayed, and the landlord started sending eviction notices.

Three months later, it looked like it was all over. They were out of cash, their employees were gone and their office had been vacated. The platform still existed, but no major new transactions or sign-ups were either taking place or on the horizon. Divakar and Ankush were back to the coffee shop and drawing board, wondering what they could have done better, faster, earlier, smarter, cheaper so ProcessBazaar could have been the success it was meant to be. They both agreed that they had a winning model and should have succeeded. It is then, that Ankush suggested, 'Should we speak to Arun again? He may have a way out for us.'

They met Arun the following morning for coffee. He came straight to the point. 'You seem to have exhausted all options and run out of steam. I hear you also let go of the three smart kids who were getting things going for you.'

'Yes, Arun. We did not secure adequate funding and were a little unwise with our spends,' Ankush volunteered.

'Divakar, what is your assessment? Do you agree?' Arun asked.

'I feel that we were a little foolish in the way we went about the business, and we lacked the ability to distinguish the need to invest from that of an expense mindset,' Divakar admitted.

'You may be right on that one. I think I understand what is happening here, and want to give you two some food for thought. Mull over what I have to say, and if it makes sense to you, then come back to me and we can attempt to resurrect ProcessBazaar.'

'When you start a company,' Arun began, 'you need to be clear on what your available start-up capital is and have an agreed allocation for product development and business development. Doing one and not doing the other is a ticket for failure.

'Growth of the business is the key mantra and must be supported at all costs in the early stages, till you cross the hump. Giving up too early makes the best of product companies fail; you are no different.

'Your first few employees will determine the future of the

venture. You need to nurture, handhold, support, cheer and egg them on like no tomorrow. Giving up and not being there, for whatever justifiable reasons, is a no-no.

'There are no shortcuts in a start-up and no either-or options. You need to commit yourselves to it and burn your bridges, if any. Holding on to a job while waiting for your start-up to scale does not work.

'You must have a contingency fund, and a plan B and plan C in the early stages. Things can and will go wrong, and you need to have the ability and intent to address problems as they crop up. Assuming things won't go wrong, or waiting for something to happen before doing something about it is sub-optimal and can lead to the business shutting down.

'As I've said before, don't cut off your nose to spite your face. While bootstrapping is a must, smart bootstrapping is even more critical. Certain costs are investments in the early stages. Have the courage and maturity to understand them and deal with them.

'Remaining adequately funded is one of the critical requirements in the early stages, and the two of you should also ensure you have a 50 per cent contingency fund as a back-up. If you need ₹3 crore, plan for ₹4.5 crore.

'And finally, timing is of the essence. A few lakh rupees at the right time is more valuable than ten times the money after the downslide. You will now need to put in at least a crore to get things back on track, and all for the want of ₹10 lakh rupees earlier.'

Divakar and Ankush couldn't disagree with any of Arun's points. He had provided an eloquent and succinct summarization of where they had gone wrong; the good news was that it only reinforced their faith in their business idea and re-energized them to try again.

They decided to start immediately. Ankush wrote out his letter of resignation and sent it to his company. Divakar got in touch with their three erstwhile employees to convince them to return. They then put together a list of friends who could invest ₹10 lakh rupees each in their venture, and started setting up meetings with them to discuss their proposition. The landlord of the office was called and persuaded to lease the space to them again; fortunately, it was still unoccupied.

At the end of five hours of non-stop working on their laptops, they had both come to one conclusion: their venture was doable, and they had taken the first step.

They shut shop long past midnight, tired, but with a sparkle in their eyes. As they walked out of Starbucks, they looked at each other and said, 'Let's do it!'

Justifying Means To What End

Giridhar Kedia had inherited a small plot of land from his father on the outskirts of Mumbai and over the past decade, had created a niche for himself amongst the mushrooming residential property developers as a reliable and trustworthy builder for the middle class segment of Navi Mumbai. His business model centred on solid and reliable construction at reasonable prices and timely delivery, which resonated well with the populace of the metropolis. He prided himself on the fact that he had remained true to his commitments and had delivered on his projects, absorbing all the challenges and travails of the industry himself.

He was developing his fifth project, an ambitious gated community that comprised 1,500 apartments, spread over seven tall structures housed in 75 acres of land located conveniently along the Mumbai-Panvel highway. It was the biggest such development that anyone had attempted. The complex, with its clubhouse, school, hospital and gardens all laid out within a beautifully and thoughtfully designed space, was one of its kind and drew customers and investors alike by the droves.

Then had come the global financial crisis; real estate was greatly impacted by the cascading effect of the global meltdown. Prices had crashed, sales were down to a trickle, the banks had tightened their purse strings and the rising consumer backlash had caused the first signs of litigation and adverse pressures on the industry. Giridhar had somehow managed to keep his head above water, but now he was desperate. His dream township, Pride Estates from his company Pride Realty was at a stage where he needed cash to keep the construction machinery running and retain the customer credibility he had so painstakingly built over a decade. He was acutely aware that maintaining his image and credibility was of prime importance in these testing times.

He had been diligently exploring all avenues of securing financing for the project, including banks, fund houses, friends, large industrialists and their private investment offices, but the times were such that not much help was forthcoming. He was even referred to a few dubious businessmen, who had asked him to hand over the project in toto to them for a meagre ₹100 crore. He had obviously turned them down and had continued his search for the light at the end of the tunnel. Today had been the last straw. His regular banker, who had solidly backed him for the past ten years, had politely turned down his request for financing, saying that they had hit their limit of sectoral exposure on real estate. He was at his wit's end and was contemplating who or where he should turn to.

His phone rang, interrupting his thoughts. Not many people had his private number, and he looked at the screen to see his friend Sunny Bhagnani's name flashing.

'Hey man, what's up?' His schoolmate Sunny's voice boomed from the other end. Giridhar and Sunny had stayed in touch though Sunny had relocated to Delhi where he was now working as the construction and operations head for a new real estate company in the NCR region.

'Hi Sunny, how come you suddenly remembered me? It's been a while since I heard from you.'

'How's the real estate magnate doing? Continuing to make waves in the Navi Mumbai market, I hear,' Sunny responded.

Sunny had been a typical Delhi boy when they were in college: loud, boisterous, handsome and forever chasing girls. He was a good bloke at heart, though, thought Giridhar.

Sunny came to the point, breaking his train of thought. 'I will be in Mumbai tomorrow and wanted to catch up with you. Times are tough, and our company recently benefitted from a source of funding; I will be meeting the funders to explore if they can give us another tranche to tide things over. Maybe you would like to join me for the meeting. Who knows, they may fund you as well,' Sunny added as a joke.

Giridhar, who was willing to clutch at any straws, promptly agreed to meet Sunny and go to the meeting as well.

They met at the airport and drove to the outskirts of the city, beyond Kalyan, to a village called Poisar, and on to a farmhouse in the middle of nowhere.

Giridhar asked Sunny, 'I hope you know where we are going and what we are doing here?'

Sunny smiled and said, 'You forget I have been here before, successfully negotiated a deal and funded our project.'

They were greeted at the door by Amol, who appeared to be the major-domo of the farmhouse and who clearly knew Sunny.

'Sunnyji, kaise ho? Sahib is waiting,' so saying, he ushered them into an air-conditioned lounge with plush carpeting and comfortable sofas where a young help was busy filling glasses with cold water.

They met Mr Waghmare, a portly, sinister-looking gentleman dressed in white kurta and pyjamas, with a pair of Ray-Bans shielding his eyes. After exchanging pleasantries, they got down to discussing the business at hand. Sunny expressed his need for ₹10 crore; the terms were agreed at 12 per cent interest with the loan for a period of five years. Giridhar's jaw dropped. He had never heard of these rates for a loan, especially when even banks were operating at over 15 per cent, with collateral support. The next thing that came as a shock to him was that fact that 40 per cent of the loan would be in cash, delivered to an address in Delhi provided by Sunny's company. Sunny seemed very comfortable and confident that it was all above board, and even the strange request for a blank agreement to be signed as security, with a demand for stamp duty of 8 per cent to be paid up front, did not seem to faze him.

Mr Waghmare then turned his attention to Giridhar. 'Aren't you also a developer? I keep hearing your name in Navi Mumbai. You are doing good work.'

He nodded his head vigorously a few times, to signify ratification and a pat on the back.

'How is your business doing? Is the township sold out? Are you on schedule to deliver next March? I hear construction has come to a standstill. Anything we can do to help?'

For Giridhar, those words were like manna from heaven. He grabbed at the apparent opportunity presented. He immediately responded, 'Yes, we are stuck for want of capital. I need a very large amount to get going again.'

'How much?' questioned the pockmarked gentleman from

behind the comfort of his Ray-Bans.

'We need ₹60 crore to tide over the crisis,' replied Giridhar.

There was a period of uncomfortable silence while Mr Waghmare contemplated the figure quoted and Giridhar squirmed, regretting his disclosure.

'We can help you,' Mr Waghmare finally said. 'But you need to arrange ₹2 crore as stamp duty and processing charges immediately. You will also submit all the original papers for the project, the land ownership and approvals, which we shall retain as collateral till you repay our loan. The papers will be kept with our lawyers in escrow. We can even consider a neutral lawyer, if you so want.'

This comforted Giridhar, and he started leaning towards accepting the proposal in spite of the warning bells over the ₹2 crore ringing in his ears.

'I accept the terms. Please tell me what the next steps are,' he enthusiastically queried.

'Please deliver ₹2 crore in cash to the Vashi Four Points Sheraton tomorrow. We will call you with the details. It has been a pleasure doing business with you. All the best and please complete and deliver your ambitious project on time.'

The meeting concluded with another round of pleasantries and goodbyes all around.

Sunny and he exchanged few words on the way back. Although they knew little about his background and the company he represented, both were thanking the powers above for the good fortune of having met Mr Waghmare. After dropping Sunny off at the airport, Giridhar got busy arranging the ₹2 crore. Precisely at 10.00 a.m. the following morning he got a call from Mr Waghmare who told him a Mr Patil would be waiting for him at the coffee shop of the Four Points Sheraton.

The meeting was scheduled for 3.00 p.m., and Giridhar was specifically asked to be present to finalize the transaction.

The meeting and exchange took place at the appointed hour and within a matter of minutes, Mr Patil was gone. Giridhar returned to his office and got busy with the day-to-day challenges for the rest of his day.

Two days later, his alarm bells started to ring. There had been no news from Mr Waghmare or his cronies. He tried calling the landline number Mr Waghmare had called him from to set up the exchange, only to find that it was the telephone number of a local merchant in Kalyan. He called Sunny, who was equally stressed. He had delivered ₹50 lakh to a courier in Delhi. It was then that Sunny disclosed the fact that their previous transaction for a crore was only partially funded, to the tune of ₹25 lakh, and the balance was to have been delivered the day before.

Giridhar decided to take matters into his own hands and kicked himself for falling for what he was now convinced was a well-engineered scam. He sent his people to the farmhouse after drawing out a map for them. They returned and told him that it was locked and belonged to an NRI who had purchased it a few weeks ago. The papers and records for the purchase were in order. The seller was a well-known industrialist from the area and Giridhar's call to him only confirmed his suspicions. The industrialist had sold the property through the lawyers of the buyer, who were the biggest in the business in Mumbai. It was a dead end. So much for the confidence, the knowledge and process orientation, the escrow and lawyers, the apparent awareness of his reputation; it had all been a very well and slickly executed scam, Giridhar realized.

A dejected and beaten Giridhar was sitting in his office with his head in his hands when his phone rang.

'Mr Kedia, this is Ranganathan from GreenBuild Funds. We are interested in venture funding a line of debt to your company. Can we meet this evening to take things forward?'

Given his current mindset, Giridhar immediately said, 'I want to check your credentials if you do not mind, Mr Ranganathan. Let me get back to you. Can you email me some information about your organization? Once bitten twice shy, you know.'

This mysterious sentence, Giridhar realized, could jeopardize things if not corrected. So he quickly added, 'I do get random calls offering us money; I hope you understand.'

Fortunately, things turned out to be above board. A week later, he had completed the process, had a written commitment for ₹50 crore, and his project was back in full swing. He had also helped Sunny by loaning him ₹1 crore from his personal account. It was then that he sat back and thought about the eventful two weeks just gone by. For the first time in his career, he had attempted to follow the credo of 'the ends justify the means,' added quotes and fixed the general saying, and did he get burnt. He resolved to never again go anywhere near such transactions. He knew real estate as a sector was prone to such scams, and wrote off the ₹2 crore he had paid in cash as an education for himself.

Controlled Risks And Managed Growth

Raghavendra Bhatt was very excited. He had just concluded a deal that allowed him 'Own and Lease' of equipment worth ₹3 crore to an amusement park in Rajasthan as an operating lease. Rags, as he was known, was thrilled as he had managed to deploy the entire capital surplus, barring expenses provisioning for twelve months, on leasing, the core proposition of his company. He now had, he proudly preened to himself, a list of nine customers with leased equipment worth ₹10 crore generating, as he was fond of saying, a return of 35 per cent, ensuring the business made handsome profits in cash. 'Not a bad beginning for someone who everyone assumed did not know how to successfully run a business as he never run one before!' he rehearsed the line that he would use in all public and private forums in the months to come.

The story began about two years ago, when he and his schoolmate and friend, Anjali Markande, had gotten together over a cup of coffee to crib about the fact that they were the backroom boys who worked their butts off to generate profits and valuation for their company, a leading financial technology service provider in Pune. In fact, the company had, on the back of their domain knowledge and the platform they had helped build, secured an investment of US $50 million from a global Private Equity fund, thus putting the valuation of the three-year-old company at US $300 million. The twenty employees of the company had shot to fame overnight, and the media had splashed their promoters' names and photos everywhere, making them mini-celebrities. Anjali and Rags had, on the spur of the moment, decided that they would both quit and get into business for themselves.

They had both worked in the financial services space, albeit in risk and technology support, but were aware of the opportunities the sector provided in the rapidly developing economy. A chance encounter with an entrepreneur who ran a printing business had convinced Rags of the great opportunity that leasing equipment to SMEs in India provided; the bankers did not like the space, and the non-banking financial companies did not understand leasing well enough to convince customers of the value of doing so. He had shared his thoughts with Anjali, and she had endorsed the view that leasing was a better risk to take than unsecured debt, which was the default product for the SME sector. They decided to take the plunge by investing their own savings and started the RAAN Leasing Company in October 2014.

They got lucky to start with. Once their colleagues and friends heard about their venture and spent an hour listening to Raghavendra's passionate exposition on the opportunities and merits of leasing, they had commitments for capital contributions pouring in. They soon managed to garner ₹4 crore and commitments for another ₹5 crore twelve months down the line. Their game had kicked off in the best way possible; they had an investible surplus of ₹5 crore to begin with. They rented a small but well-furnished office in one of the upper middle commercial complexes in Pune and soon they and their core team of six employees were ready to open their doors for business.

They officially started operations on 26 January 2015, with the blessings and support of their parents and well-wishers. The first few months were spent putting together the business development plan and getting their back-end systems ready for the first leasing transaction. They had divided the responsibilities between themselves: Anjali took charge of operations, risk and accounting, while Rags kept business development, marketing and public relations, investor relations and external interfaces with himself. They soon settled into a rhythm, and the office started looking like that of a successful early-stage enterprise, humming with activity and with a buoyant and upbeat team.

They signed their first customer after ten rejections from a risk perspective. It was a restaurant seeking to open at a new location and with the goal of creating a chain of quick service restaurants, or QSRs, as they were known. Anjali and Rags evaluated, verified and approved the amount of ₹50 lakh for the kitchen and central kitchen equipment, and they were revenue generating by July 2015. Soon, they had a variety of businesses, all falling within the SME gamut, from leather accessory manufacturers to printing concerns, from gyms to packaging units, applying to them for funding for leasing machinery, given the fact that these SMEs could convert their capital outlay requirements to an operating expense, thus saving them the stress of raising chunks of capital. Both Anjali and Rags were conscientious and dedicated to ensuring they did not approve any high-risk deals.

By the time they had approved eight clients for funding their equipment, they had deployed about 60 per cent of the capital they had managed to raise.

Very soon, they were down to their last few crores, and Rags realized that he would have to hit the streets to raise the next round of capital. With the signing of the deal with their ninth client they had deployed their last ₹3 crore to Desert Drive Entertainment, an amusement park set up outside Jaisalmer that rented dirt and sand bikes and 4 Wheel Drive desert vehicles to tourists. It promised to be a hugely lucrative business given the tourist inflow to Rajasthan. Anjali and Rags got together with their team to celebrate their new client, and as the evening progressed, they toasted themselves for proving their detractors wrong. Both were already thinking ahead of how they would raise the next round of capital of US $25 million conservatively, and leverage the same to create a ₹500 crore; a cool ₹50 crore bottom-line business, and the fame and visibility to go with it.

As the next few months went by, however, the dream slowly started disintegrating. Rags' efforts to meet potential investors and fund houses had met with initial interest but all his leads had petered out to polite rejections. It soon became apparent that the next round of capital raising was going to be a serious challenge. Anjali and Rags spent hours trying to figure out why, in spite of their clean set of clients, no delinquencies, ₹10 crore of investment in leased assets, low-cost structures and strong technology support and software, they were not the darling of the investment community; it made no sense to them. To add to their woes, one of their earliest investments had started to stutter and was behind on their payments by a few months.

Over the next six months, things went from bad to worse. The earliest investment was now into litigation for recovery, and their latest baby, the desert amusement business, hit summer, the lean season for tourists. The lease payments stopped coming, and Rags was forced to spend fifteen days a month trying to get Desert Drive Entertainment to cough up enough to keep the account within the limits of being classified as delinquent. They were running three months behind schedule, and the picture did not look like it would improve any time soon. Anjali suggested they seek professional help to relook at their strategy and approach to growth, and figure out a way to salvage the business before they went belly-up.

Rags had to bite the bullet and agree. They were advised to seek the help of Arpan Gupta, a well-known professional in the business consulting space who was regarded as the person to go to for strategic inputs. Their ex-boss, who had worked with Arpan in the past, helped them set up a meeting and they drove to Mumbai to meet him.

All this was running through their minds, as they waited for Arpan in his office, and Anjali and Rags were both very apprehensive. They were secretly dreading the thought that they may well be asked to shut the business down, given their set of challenges.

Arpan walked in, cheerful, and greeted them with warm handshakes. 'So, the leasing kings are here. That is what your ex-boss Subodh calls you,' he said with a smile. 'I have been through the note you sent me but would like to hear your story in detail. Can you run me through the chain of events, with the thinking behind everything you did?'

Anjali and Rags took turns to explain their story from how

they began to where they were today. They had also put together a presentation on their company's financials and the business parameters and highlights as they existed. Arpan went through it rapidly, with no comment. He then took a few minutes to make some notes in his scribble pad and then looked up.

'You have driven the business into a difficult situation. But I believe it can be salvaged and put back on track. You will, however, need to take a few tough calls and execute all that I advise. It's a classic mistake that I have seen several entrepreneurs make to show rapid growth and progress.'

He paused and Anjali and Rags nodded, encouraging him to go on.

He continued, 'It's advisable to begin small and then scale up in terms of the products and sector risks that you take in the leasing business. Nine customers for ₹10 crore of assets leased is an inverted pyramid. I am surprised that a risk professional could even contemplate this.

'Given the capitalization and limited bandwidth, the segments you have leased to are the last I would have considered. Each asset category is a high-risk one, and the repossession possibilities and resale values do not exist there. The more standard categories, such as medical equipment, SME machinery of wider use, and the better-understood industry segments should have been the first assets to fund.

'The residual value of any asset that you fund should be one of the key considerations for asset financing under lease. It forms a critical part of your criteria for financing the assets. I don't see that in the current scenario.

'Begin with sectors you understand and geographies that are more accessible in terms of ability to reach and influence under adverse circumstances. You seem to have missed that as well.

'Seasonal and skewed cash flow businesses, by definition, are a lot riskier. Keep them out of your potential client list.

'Cash-centric businesses, where the cash flow can be presented the way one wants to, is another area where one needs to show caution. The cash flow statements can never be predicted, nor used to justify either payments or delays.

'The key to managing growth is to manage and control the risks. To this end, you should gradually scale up and build a diversified portfolio of clients targeting businesses that you understand in regions and markets that are more accessible. Entrepreneurs who have been in the business for a while with strong roots in the regional industry and interdependences, B2C non-seasonal businesses, these are ideal in the initial days. As your portfolio grows, your appetite for risk should also grow.

'Esoteric, chunky, environment-specific assets are at the other end of the spectrum; you should fund them only when you can afford to take those risks. Anyway, concentration risk norms of not more than 5 per cent of gross value of the portfolio in one asset exposure and a similar cap on the one business exposure are strongly recommended going forward.'

All this was lapped up by the two budding enthusiasts, and they looked enquiringly at Arpan, as if asking, 'What do we do now?'

Arpan, sensing their query, continued.

'Close the case of the first asset you funded; get a settlement whereby you are at least able to repossess the asset. Sell it at distress value and exit. You have already recovered your cost of the asset in the lease rentals collected so far.

'Go down to Rajasthan and downsize the asset exposure. Pick up half the number of bikes and four-wheelers you have funded; speak to the supplier and figure out how you can sell them to someone else on their potential buyers list. The assets are not very old, and the likelihood of more entrepreneurs jumping onto this business bandwagon is high.

'Reduce your exposure and lease rentals due from this customer, and renegotiate the terms of the lease and pricing. He will be willing to do so, given that Rags has a great relationship with the borrower.

'Redeploy the money into smaller value assets and increase your customer base to between 30-50 customers; start making the sectoral and single client exposures move towards the internal standards outlined.

'Over the next six months, please do not seek to either raise capital or debt. Let's get the portfolio looking far healthier, and better managed before you put yourselves out there.

'I notice that you have enough cash to meet the burn for at least another twelve months; keep your costs where they are, or try and shave off a few lakhs per month. It will lead to better operating ratios.

'All this will enable you to position yourself as a company well on the road to a turnaround. If an investor asks, I would advise you to accept the fact that you made mistakes but did a course correction and are now back on track. Honesty is a great trait in an entrepreneur and any investor worth his salt knows that. So let's get cracking and put this leasing train back on its tracks!'

Anjali and Raghavendra left Arpan's office feeling lighter and more cheerful and optimistic than they had in the last twelve months. They were confident that the insights and knowledge they had acquired were their ticket to turnaround and success.

Scaling Highs And Lows

Subrat and Indrani Dasgupta were on their way to Ooty for a well-earned break when Subrat's phone buzzed ominously. This was the first time in a year that they had taken a few days off to relax after the crazy period of whirlwind travel, hard negotiations, aggressive expansion, rampant hiring and simultaneous setting up of new units in new towns. Their venture, Being Indian Enterprises, had been an all-consuming effort over the past twelve months.

About eighteen months ago, they had secured an infusion of significant capital, which had been beyond even their own ambitions, from the venture fund, VentureBig. They had received US $15 million in funding to scale up and expand their quick service restaurant (QSR) chain, 'Being Indian', from three units in Kolkata to forty units across India. The ball, set rolling by the infusion and the vision they had created, had led to a mad rush and a period of intense activity, culminating in the last opening a few days ago in Bengaluru. They had unanimously decided to take some time off to recharge their batteries and take another look at their business goals and objectives to make sure they had not missed anything.

Subrat and Indrani had been neighbours in the small town of Kharagpur and had schooled together. They had both subsequently gone their separate ways, but coincidentally both had pursued catering and culinary arts as careers, and they had met again when they were doing a stint together at one of the leading hotel chains in India. Their friendship had blossomed into love and they had tied the knot in 1998. Today, about sixteen years later, they were in their fourth year as partners in crime, as they jokingly referred to their venture, running a successful chain of QSRs conceived over a quiet night of drinks and dinner four years ago. Subrat was the high energy, leading from the front kind of chef, encouraging and pushing his teams to go the extra mile, while Indrani was all grace and poise, rational, logical, thinking through and probing every aspect of the business. They made a great team; their complementary skills and the intuitive understanding and communication between them had proved to be an asset in the world of brutal reality that was India.

Their concept restaurant, serving Indian food with a modern twist, had struck a chord with the millennial generation and the young and progressive Indian middle- and upper-middle class of customers. Generous and flattering write-ups thanks to Subrat's charm and ease with journalists and his great culinary skills had started drawing crowds to their restaurant, beyond even their own optimistic estimates. They had both seen the opportunity to expand within Kolkata and had opened two more units, one in Salt Lake City and the other on Rash Behari Avenue, apart from the first one on Park Street. It was during this phase of high-intensity branding and public relations that they had caught the attention of VentureBig, a leading Venture Capital Fund, as well as of the local political bigwigs who wanted a slice of their success.

It had been a period of intense learning for them; they were exposed to the nuances of capital raising, which was Greek and Latin to them, and to the not-so-fair and transparent political overtures, which again was something they had not encountered before. Indrani and Subrat had dealt with both of these challenges themselves, stumbling, faltering, but picking themselves up till they had ironed out a long-term approach and way of working with both these animals. The politicos had eased off after Subrat and Indrani had approached the leader of the political party, who had subsequently sent a subtle message to his cohorts to leave the duo alone. They had had to cater to special parties and banquet requests from the bigwigs from time to time, but had agreed that it was a small price to pay for the relative non-interference.

On the capital raising, however, they had not been as lucky. VentureBig had been relentless, pushing them to accept a large amount of money, which both were reluctant to do. Ramesh Reddy, the managing partner, had gone out of his way to give them what appeared to be a very juicy deal, and as a consequence, the generous sum of ₹100 crore had found its way into their capital of which some went into their pockets as well. But they had not bargained for the pressure that accepting the funding would bring on growth and expansion. Ramesh had started to exert subtle and not-so-subtle pressure on them to scale the business, and while Indrani and Subrat had tried to reason with him and push back, they were not very successful in doing so. The net result was a mad phase of expansion, negotiation, travel, late nights, hiring, firing and capital purchases, not all of which was to their liking. They were uncomfortable with some of the choices they had been forced to make and compromises were made in the effort to meet the business plan objectives. They had reluctantly agreed to this business plan as part of the capital infusion and shareholders' agreement.

It seemed like yesterday that they had embarked on this roller coaster ride, and it was only now that they were taking the time to breathe and take stock of their business in its entirety.

The phone ringing again brought Subrat back to reality. 'Subrat, we have a problem!' the accepted number three in the organization, Ravindran's voice echoed from the other end. 'Our restaurants in NCR have a serious issue of embezzlement, and what's worse, I am fairly sure it is a widespread malaise that has affected other branches as well.'

Subrat gave one of the ear pieces of his earphones to Indrani so she could listen in on the conversation. 'Our cash sales, which used to comprise about 50 per cent of sales revenues in each of our four restaurants, are now down to 15 per cent while the overall revenue numbers seem to have dropped to 60 per cent of their normal volumes. Demonetization had hit us, but even at its peak, the drop was not as drastic in terms of cash sales and overall revenues.'

Indrani signalled to Subrat, asking him to check on consumption and purchases, which he conveyed to Ravindran.

'The purchase and consumption numbers I have received do not show any reduction. I have asked Jain to look at the numbers in detail,' Ravindran responded to the query.

Jain was their key accounts man, a long-serving, loyal and

trusted lieutenant whose integrity was above board.

Subrat looked at Indrani and they both nodded in silent agreement. 'We are going to Delhi immediately; please ask Ruma to cancel our hotel reservation in Ooty and book us on this evening's flight to Delhi from Bengaluru. We have both been concerned about the pace of growth and what we have been pushing ourselves towards. Our fears seem to be coming true,' Subrat said to Ravindran before hanging up.

They were both lost in thought throughout the journey back to Bengaluru; Indrani was running through the events that had preceded their launch in NCR: the desperate race for meeting the deadlines for launch, Ramesh's incessant pushing, the brief interviews and discussions via Skype, the lack of properly referenced candidates and the selection of Navin Taneja as the head for the operations in NCR. Navin had come to them through an agency, and they had not had the time to check his references; he seemed to have worked in quite a few fine dining restaurants and QSRs, and had also worked in a few hotels, but she could not recollect a single long stint in his track record. Her logical mind started thinking through how the crime could have been pulled off. She said to Subrat, 'Can you please speak to Atul Khosla, of Oh Baluchi, and check with him on Navin? I seem to remember he worked for Atul in the past. I think the embezzlement can only be happening with Navin's connivance and knowledge. It's good to go prepared.'

Subrat agreed with her and immediately called Atul. After an exchange of pleasantries, he got to the point. 'Atul, do you remember Navin? I believe he worked for you. I just wanted to check with you what you thought of him.'

There was a pointed silence for a good thirty seconds.

'Why? Are you planning to hire him? I can only say he

knows his job, maybe a little too well,' Atul finally responded.

Subrat's antennae went up. 'What do you mean by that?' he probed.

'Well, we had to let him go as he was found guilty of being a SHIT case, a short hand in the till,' was Atul's reluctant admission, after a bit of probing and prodding.

Subrat thanked him and hung up. Armed with this knowledge, he knew their digging into facts would be a little easier as they got down to assessing the rot and initiated the clean-up.

On the flight to Delhi, Indrani and Subrat chalked out their action plan. Navin had not been informed about their visit as they knew any warning of their arrival would lead to a scramble to suppress facts and destroy evidence. They wanted a chance to see for themselves the occupancy and working of their restaurants.

They both knew that finding evidence of wrongdoing would require some digging and investigation. So they decided to call their friend, philosopher and guide, Satyen Sahoo, who had been instrumental in educating them on the running of a successful business and had hand-held them through the capital infusion stage. However, Ramesh Reddy had not liked his involvement, and they had been forced to subtly distance themselves from him. Their own respect and admiration for Satyen had not, however, reduced in any way as a consequence.

Satyen was a doyen of the industry, having built successful businesses across domains over three decades. An alumnus of one of the premier engineering institutes, he also held a postgraduate degree from the premier management institute of India, IIM Ahmedabad. Over the past six years, he had built a successful consulting business focused on guiding businesses from concept to scale and helping them negotiate the changing topography of challenges and issues along the way. He had, been introduced to Indrani and Subrat by friends and had in a very short period, made a lasting impression on them. They had both felt guilt and remorse when they had had to cut short their engagement with Satyen and his company, rather abruptly, a year ago.

Indrani was the one who made the call once they landed in Delhi and were on the way to the Oberoi in Gurgaon.

'Hi, Indrani. What a pleasant surprise! So good to hear from you after all this while. Hope both of you are doing well.'

Indrani decided to be upfront with him. 'Thank you, Satyen. We are both fine and have just landed in Delhi. I was wondering if we could ask you to spare some time for us tomorrow, early, over breakfast, if possible. We need your guidance and advice on some serious issues we are grappling with.'

'Sure, 8.00 a.m. tomorrow. Where can I meet you guys? Where are you staying?'

They decided to meet at the Oberoi and Indrani hung up with a polite thank you, leaving the rest of the conversation for the morrow.

The next morning, in the pleasant environs of the Oberoi, in a quiet corner, Subrat and Indrani were having an intense conversation with Satyen. They quickly brought him up to speed on the company and its happenings over the past year or so, and then described the current challenge they were facing. Satyen heard them out quietly, and after a brief pause, while coffee was served, he voiced his opinions.

'I am going to tell you what my understanding of the issues are and what I think the two of you should do. However, my understanding is based on the gleanings from our conversation, and may be limited in perspective. I suggest the two of you deliberate on what I have to say and then decide to execute some, or all of my suggestions, if it makes sense to do so.'

Indrani and Subrat nodded their agreement.

'Very well, here's how I see it. Your business model was always a challenge, and as you scaled, controls and checks and balances became more critical to success. I believe you have compromised rigour at the altar of growth.

'I had expressed this when you accepted the capital infusion from VentureBig. The expansion and growth plans were a little too ambitious. Going to fifty restaurants in two years meant opening two restaurants a month, and that kind of pace was not advisable or sustainable with the quality standards you had set for yourselves.

'Ramesh and his team are investors, for whom the return on investment is paramount. Given the funding they made available, I had warned you that they would drive you guys very hard to ensure growth, profitability and returns. I think you bit off more than you could reasonably chew.

'In the restaurant business, cash is intrinsic to daily revenues and growth, especially in India. Hence, it is of prime importance to have a complete handle on the cash inflows and outflows, every day. I do not see that degree of monitoring in the present set-up. It's a negative working capital business; it will generate more cash than you spend, and hence any leakages are harder to find and arrest.

'The primary criteria for choosing your team, therefore, have to be integrity and honesty. Any other competencies can only follow. I remember advising you two to ensure you conducted thorough background checks on every hire. Better be safe than sorry.

'Exception management is the way to go as you scale. Hence, any blip must come to your notice within twenty-four hours of its occurrence. A month cannot go by before red flags are raised, which seems to be the case here.

'Standardization and consumption tracking are the key to success here. Your central kitchens should play a pivotal role once they are set up. The NCR one failed here, apparently, or colluded, as we need to discover. I am sure you have defined processes for the same and investigations will expose the truth.

'Security measures should include cameras as well as cash and till controls. I am sure you have them; if not, install them on priority across all outlets.

'In a flow business, which is what your QSR business is, you cannot afford operations to be at a standstill. Clientele once lost takes a long time to recover and can even lead to closure of the outlets. So, do everything you must without stopping or slowing the business.

'Take your time in finding replacements for the people who you may find guilty. You need to be doubly sure of the integrity of the person in charge. You cannot afford a second incident; it will mean the closure of all operations in NCR.

'I suggest that you get your finance guys to Delhi and start an audit of all units and the central kitchen. Check purchases, consumption patterns, payments, cash accounting and withdrawals from the bank accounts. It will help identify the degree of the malaise.

'Kitchen Orders (KOTs), billing at each outlet and the end-of-day uploads will also throw some light on the events. Observe one full day's behaviour to get a fix on the occupancy and turnaround of tables, with billings.

'Make Ravindran the city head of the business in the interim.

Subrat, you can take on his role till you find a replacement for Navin, who I presume will be the first to go.

'Start getting all your centres audited, across cities, on priority. The rot could have spread everywhere. You do not have time to waste. Indrani, I suggest you personally supervise this.

'With regard to the Delhi team, confront them with data. Do not go in blind. I suggest you brief Ramesh a few days later, after you have taken concrete action to rectify and arrest the leak.

Satyen paused here and looked at the two of them thoughtfully before continuing.

'I am sure you will come out of this with minor bruises; there is nothing here that firm action cannot fix. But you need to address a broader strategy issue. The pace of growth you have set for yourselves leaves you vulnerable to such execution failures. It can push you to take shortcuts in rigour and process, which can have far-reaching consequences.

'You will need to confront Ramesh and his team with the facts and recast your business expectations. While it may not be what they want, I am sure he will understand that managed growth is critical to ensuring longevity and returns. A slowdown and consolidation at this stage will only position you better for the next phase of growth.

'Do not worry about how your investor will react under the circumstances. Whenever an entrepreneur is funded, the funding is very much for the value and passion that the promoter brings to the table. In most cases, investors take a gamble on the promoters, which is both of you, and not so much on the business per se.

'It may also be an opportune time to table the fact that you may actually have more capital than you need, especially in a high EBITDA, negative working capital business. Do not get pushed into inorganic growth and acquisitions, consequently. Push back and seek a recalibration of expectations and outcomes.

'Let me know if I can be of any further help. All the best, and I am sure things will fall into place very quickly,' Satyen said before taking his leave and walking out of the coffee shop.

Indrani and Subrat looked relieved; Satyen had given them a very good perspective on the issues facing their business and some valuable insights on how to handle the situation.

They walked out of the Oberoi confident in the belief that together, they had it in themselves to get over this minor bump, and move ahead with faith and confidence. There was also the added comfort of knowing that they had someone like Satyen to lean on for advice and support. Both of them said a silent prayer of Thanks, glad they had not burnt their bridges with him earlier.

The Valuation Trap

Vishal Kapoor was waiting in his office for Sumathi Ramachandran, with whom he had sought a meeting. He and his partner Nisha Jaiswal had heard her address a gathering of start-up CEOs and had related to her views on growth, profits, scale and valuations. They themselves were grappling with a dilemma that they had been unable to resolve. The session, very well attended and appreciated, had ratified their belief that they needed a sounding board to bounce their thoughts off and a mentor to hand-hold them through the dichotomous phase that their company, E-ShopEase, was going through. As a result, Vishal had called Sumathi's office to set up a meeting with her. She had agreed and had suggested that the meeting take place in their office as she believed it would give her a better idea of their team and business.

Vishal was one of the millennial youngsters who had decided to be an entrepreneur after a short stint in the IT industry about five years previously. He had, along with his colleague Nisha, conceptualized an online marketplace focused on electronics, computers and the like. They had together bootstrapped the same, and thanks to some very generous uncles and aunts on both sides, had managed to adequately fund themselves and soon had a budding business going. Over the past five years, they had scaled their company to an ₹800-crore business, and unlike most players in the market, had created a healthy post tax profit of ₹160 crore as well.

Things had been hunky-dory till the advent of major players like Amazon and Flipkart, which had quickly nullified their uniqueness and started the squeeze on their profitability. However, the crux of the issue was the challenge of funding the growth and ensuring the business continued to scale, thus positioning it as an ideal acquisition target, which both of them firmly believed it to be. In their desire to do so, both Nisha and Vishal had stretched themselves and tried all options and ploys to retain their brands, their customers and their profitability. But their efforts did not produce the desired results. At best, they had managed to keep their profits at the last financial year's levels, with a 25 per cent growth in revenues.

That had been the story till about nine months ago. That is, it was the story till they had suddenly been flooded with calls from several private equity funds as well as some of their competitors, all of whom were interested in investing in them or buying them out. It had all started with an interview on CNBC, where they were featured as a hot and upcoming online business. When asked whether they would be amenable to an investment or acquisition, both had in unison said 'Yes'. That had opened the floodgates. Every single source and mode of investment and every one of their local representatives, had made a beeline for their offices. Very soon, they were in serious discussions with at least three potential buyers or investors, and things had moved to a stage where the term sheet was being negotiated clause by clause.

That was when their own differences and approaches to risk-taking came to the forefront. Nisha was of the firm belief that a valuation in terms of a decent multiple to the revenues was adequate and a fair value for their business; Vishal, on the other hand, was constantly comparing the offers with the valuations that their better-known peers were getting and the multiples at which they had been funded. As a result, there was no meeting of minds on this count and every term sheet possibility fizzled out on hitting this deal-breaking barrier. This slowly translated into a chasm between the two and the effects started telling on the business and the company.

Revenues dropped, as did motivation and energy; employees started sensing the drift, and for the first time, members of their core team of ten started leaving, expressing a desire to move on to other ventures and start-ups. They had lost two employees, and a few more had expressed their desire to move on. Nisha and Vishal often tried to talk through their differences; but the gap was too large to bridge. It came to a point where Nisha offered to sell her stake to Vishal at what she considered a reasonable valuation and move on to setting up another venture. Vishal, of course, outright rejected her offer as he believed they could and should get a much higher price for both their stakes.

Then the world went into a correction drive; oil prices dropped, North Korea and the US started threatening each other, Brexit remained an unsettling issue, the IT industry started experiencing the H1B visa blues, and closer to home, Flipkart and others saw valuations being hammered with their biggest investors taking write-downs, and a pall of uncertainty clouded the horizon and depressed sentiments. The impact was felt by E-ShopEase as well. Their suitors suddenly became scarce and discussions that had been bullish and progressing well went into reverse gear. The net result was a growing feeling of gloom and that was when they had decided to attend the seminar at which Sumathi Ramachandran was the keynote speaker. Her insightful talk had made a deep impression on both of them, and they had decided to seek her advice on their predicament and differences.

Nisha couldn't be present at the meeting with Sumathi as she had to travel for some personal and unavoidable work, thus leaving Vishal to pick Sumathi's brains.

Sumathi arrived promptly at 11.00 a.m., as committed. After the usual pleasantries, they got down to discussing the business and the dilemma facing the company. Vishal took her through the history of the company, the partnership between Nisha and himself and the roles each had played in the company's success, and finally came down to the core issues that they were both grappling with: stay or sell, and what was a fair value either way?

Sumathi heard Vishal out patiently and then shared her views and thoughts.

'I must compliment the two of you for not losing sight of the basics of building a successful business—growth and profitability. Most online players miss the latter.

'Growth at all costs seems to be the mantra today, but I keep drawing people's attention to the dotcom days and the similar trends we saw then. As it played out, the bottom dropped out of valuations.

'My personal view is that the industry today has also taken the shape of a bubble ready to burst; the jury is still out on whether pushing customer acquisition and growth at all costs is the formula for success.

'Inflated valuations are driven by the Chinese on one side and Amazon on the other, and they both have deep pockets. Where this will end is anyone's guess. You have not taken sides and are not part of any camp so far.

It does not matter to others and neither should it to you. Many players will be sacrificed at the altar of this fight, and only niche players shall survive and come out of it relatively unscathed.

'My recommendation is to keep your eye on your business; stay profitable and accept reasonable valuations and exit when you think appropriate. Your margins will continue to be squeezed, and your customer base will continue to get eroded as the large players become multi-product, multi-segment players.

'Specialization in verticals will still have a place and you are well positioned to be there. But you will have to settle for lower growth rates, scales and profitability. So, accept that fact first.

'A bird in hand is worth millions in the bush; I believe you are being unrealistic if you expect valuations to be in line with the mega players. You have made profits, taken dividends and extracted some value already so far. In this, I agree with Nisha that you need to position yourself as a good profit-making business.

'Do not short sell; wait for the right buyer and price. A price that is about two and a half times your revenues is a good benchmark today. It will only go down further. So, take an offer that gives you that.

'I think some of the larger players with deep pockets would be ideal for you, but not the mega players. Do not have any expectations that they will approach you. Their view will be that you have sacrificed growth for profitability. Hence, you are not of the right value system.'

She smiled as she said the last few lines.

Vishal slowly digested what she had shared and realized that the perspective she had provided was a valuable one. He thanked her for her input and requested her to continue mentoring them as they worked towards a culmination of their intent to sell. She agreed and Vishal showed her out of the office, expressing his gratitude for her help and advice.

He spent the next hour on the phone with Nisha, updating her on the conversation and the suggestions that Sumathi had for them.

The meeting had positive repercussions. Nisha and Vishal's relationship improved and their chemistry was back on track; their employees felt the change and two who had planned to quit had a change of heart as well.

Nisha and Vishal now tackled potential suitors together, speaking and conveying the same expectations, hopes and aspirations, communicating the image of a well-knit, well-oiled machine. This, in turn, brought about significant shifts in the approaches of some of their suitors. Instead of a confrontationist environment, every meeting was now a collaborative one, with a much friendlier atmosphere.

Three months down the line, they had their first term sheet signed and sealed; a few months after that, they both met Sumathi at her office in Bandra.

'You really helped us clear our thinking and minds; we owe you big time,' Nisha said gratefully.

'We were floundering and had almost lost the plot,' Vishal added. 'Thank you for knocking some sense into us; I guess we as youngsters tend to get carried away by what we see around us.'

'This is a small token of our appreciation,' Nisha said as she handed over a nicely wrapped package.

Sumathi smiled as she accepted the gift and said, 'Valuation games are traps that I advise all my clients to carefully avoid. The fact remains that there will be differences and being pragmatic and accepting that fact is the first step to a successful negotiation. I am glad I could be of help in bringing you back to rational thought tracks.'

Technology Selling Paradoxes

Sridhar K.S., or SKS as he was popularly known, was struggling with his growth plan and reviewing the lack of it with his sales team. He and his long-time schoolmate Harish Shah had started a venture with a lot of hope and promise about twelve months ago. Their team of engineers and PhDs had built the business on the foundation of cutting-edge engineering and technology with wide-ranging areas of application. The only common thread they wove into it was electronics and mechanical engineering as they were all passionate about how the two could integrate to offer a range of products hitherto unseen by the industry at large. They had quickly invented and patented a few technology firsts in the renewable energy, detection and forensic support, and defence domains.

However, despite this early success and several promising meetings and interactions with government and private sector companies, they had hit a dead end as far as business and contracts were concerned. SKS, as the CEO, had attended these meetings and was convinced that there was more than a passing interest in their offerings on the technology front. So he could not understand why not one of them had culminated in a firm contract for them over the past twelve months. Both Harish and he were concerned; another six months of this and they would be nearing the end of their savings and seed capital, which is what had kept things going so far.

They had both worked in an exceptionally positioned defence research establishment in the US and had been instrumental in developing some of the latest technologies for the US armed forces. It was work such as theirs that allowed the US to continue to dominate the technology race in arms, ammunition, defence systems, guidance systems, power systems, protection systems, security systems and the anti-terrorism proactive detection and preventive systems.

They had subsequently come back to India, and, in their desire to give back to the motherland, had conceptualized and established a cutting-edge technology business.

They were firm in their belief that the timing was rights. India with its new government, the thrust on renewable energy, the modernization of the Indian armed forces, the upgrade of the Indian Railways, the commitment to electric vehicles, the anti-terrorism measures and the general buzz around the latest in technology and digitization only meant that they had a great strategic advantage. Their own grounding for over three decades in the US had also enabled them to build a network of suppliers and vendor-partners who could help them produce their prototypes by providing critical components.

All this meant that they only needed to get their first set of customers locked in, which had been easier said than done. In spite of numerous meetings, follow-up meetings and discussions, they were yet to secure even a single confirmed order for the company. It was this state of affairs that had prompted SKS to seek a review and feedback meeting with the sales team.

'All our potential customers request us for our previous track record, but we do not have any to provide,' the head of sales, Amit Bhattacharya, stated, setting the ball rolling.

'We have no other customer to give as reference,' another member piped in.

'Our prices are too high. We are charging almost twice what others are quoting,' was the next complaint.

It was a well-accepted fact that in India, clients liked to negotiate very hard on price and took a certain pleasure in doing so. It helped the purchase guys earn brownie points with their bosses.

SKS was noting down the issues as they were being aired.

'We do not have samples or literature to provide, which makes it difficult to make the sale,' was the next lament.

'Customers do not understand the product and how it is superior to what is available,' said another.

'An unknown brand is also a challenge,' chipped in another voice.

'The purchase guys do not even understand what we are offering,' was the final, matter-of-fact statement.

SKS walked out of the meeting very concerned. The challenges stated by Bhattacharya and his team needed to be addressed, he knew. He himself had not had to face this issue as in his erstwhile company they had had the privilege of being the blue-eyed boys of cutting-edge technology; but that was not the case in India. Thus he was unable to come up with answers or ways around the problem. He then suddenly remembered

Nathan P.V., the whiz kid of selling strategy who had presented at a technology seminar they had attended a while ago, talking about how to sell when one had no history, brand, image or product. It had been a very interesting and unusual talk and Nathan had held the crowd's undivided attention.

SKS decided to seek Nathan out on LinkedIn and sent him a request to connect. He heard back from him the following morning, and he then shot him an email seeking a meeting. Harish, his partner, had wholeheartedly endorsed his plan to engage Nathan's services as soon as possible, as else they would not have a business to own or run.

A week later, SKS and Harish were seated in the offices of Nathan P.V. in Bengaluru, waiting to meet the gentleman and put their problems to him. Nathan walked in at 10.30 a.m. on the dot.

His opening line was, 'What are you guys not able to sell?'

SKS and Harish required no second prompt, and they launched into a long monologue on the challenges facing their company, Power-edge Technologies.

Nathan interrupted them after about ten minutes with, 'Let me try and summarize my understanding of your problem. You are a technology start-up company designing products that are way ahead of what is currently available, next-gen products, which the sales team is not able to sell as there is no previous track record, literature, brand recognition, price point comparisons, competitive benchmarks and technology awareness, amongst the many other issues. Am I right?'

'Absolutely,' responded Harish and SKS together, grateful for his quick understanding and appreciation of the problem.

'Are you guys convinced you have the right product segments, design and prototyping capabilities, skills and expertise, and the right sales team?'

Both SKS and Harish immediately nodded in the affirmative.

'You are facing a problem that is not very common in India but is more common in developed economies. It's a classic case of product innovation not being understood and appreciated leading to a premium positioning without the brand pull to sustain it. This is a vicious cycle. The premium is a consequence of the understanding of the product, which helps build the brand, but the absence of which also creates a wrong perception of an expensive product. It's a chicken and egg situation.'

SKS and Harish were absorbing this with great attention.

'There are a few things you guys need to do to try and address this and rectify the perception challenges.'

With that, Nathan became somewhat prescriptive.

'You have to adopt a different approach to sales, different from the standard pipeline generation process that we are all accustomed to. For starters, the sales effort needs to be very targeted. Identify companies in industries where you can deliver value and focus only on them.

'Once you have shortlisted the companies, your sales effort has to begin very high up in the organization, with the CEO, president or business heads; the purchase and project guys are the wrong target audience.

'Go top down as a strategy, but then plug in the connects at all levels in the organization. You will need all of them to support you on an ongoing basis; the more established you become, the lower the level at which you need well-wishers.

'It has to be a concept selling; hence, a connect or introduction is a must. Cold calling will get you nowhere.

'Your approach has to begin with a need being addressed, with no alternative therapies for the ailment. That will position your offering as a unique product option.

'You must evaluate pilots and prototype options, with a backstop on costs, and if need be, performance assurances and penalties.

'Exclusivity of usage and rights to market as a standalone or as part of a larger assembly is something you have to put forward.

'I suggest you do proof-of-concept options as a pilot in all cases and price the same very carefully. Separate the consulting and other charges and present them as optional costs.

'Production and hand-holding should be an option in your integrated proposal. The engagement should be based on an intensive model as long-drawn interactions and negotiations will be needed to close.

'Dwell on the performance or delivery enhancement of the product and its associated revenue or cost-saving opportunities. The use of your product should have an easily demonstrable and measurable significant enhancement in performance. The focus should be on the annuity benefits of this.

'Patents and IP protection are a must; make sure you have them in place as it will give comfort to buyers. Testing and independent lab certificates are also of great help.

'Certifications from international bodies and standards are also a must as you build your product portfolio. Have a dedicated team pursuing and ensuring this.

'At the end of the day, you have to approach this on a war footing; do not compromise on the focus and involvement of key senior personnel. There is no looking back on this; ensure every call, meeting, connect and opportunity counts. It is not the volume of leads and opportunities coming your way; the focus should be on converting the few that come.'

SKS and Harish had taken frantic notes, as all that was said had made immense sense to them. They walked away from the meeting, chastened but educated on the challenges and issues that a new technology company faces, in a fast-evolving market like India.

SKS and Harish were quiet all the way back from Bengaluru; there was a lot for them to digest, assimilate, share and execute as they began their journey to make Power-edge Technologies the successful enterprise it was meant to be.

The Need To Call It Quits

Rashid Khan was deep in thought. His partner Vikram Gupte and he had just been turned down for an extension of their credit line with their long-term banker, and they were looking at the end of the road for their business. All their efforts to get fresh legs for the business by way of capital or debt had come to naught despite their earnest attempts and the support of their friends who had gladly chipped in to help get them a lifeline.

Rashid fondly remembered the day they had launched their company with a lot of pomp and fanfare. He had been in the logistics space for a long time and Vikram had been a client, providing him with a string of opportunities in the transportation space. Their acquaintance had turned into a strong friendship over a period of eight years and had finally led to a business partnership, which Rashid had initiated. The idea had dawned on them during a dinner as they were both contemplating the next steps in their respective careers. Vikram had expressed a desire to get out of the corporate world, and Rashid had earnestly and impulsively suggested that they float a transportation company together.

Vikram had jumped at the idea. They had spent a few weeks putting together the business plan, the pitch and the elements of the execution and on 24 March 2011, they had launched Vikram Logistics Services, which was a radio application based taxi and goods transport service providing both to corporate clients on a call basis, thus eliminating the need to have an operator on standby. The list of clients who had evinced interest in their company was impressive. Rashid recalled that on that day itself, forty clients had signed up for a presentation and pitch to explore the firm's offerings.

From then till today, almost four years later, it had been a roller coaster ride, but over the past two years, the dips had been devastating. They had raised venture capital funds to get the venture going, which had helped them deal with the constant demands for cash. The burn that had commenced on day one had only increased over time. Rashid wondered what they had missed and whether they could have done things differently on this journey, which looked like it had reached the end of the road. The US $5 million in venture capital funding along with the US $1 million they had raised from family and friends was almost exhausted. There was no silver lining in sight, and today was the last straw.

'Vikram, I think we should just shut the company down. We have tried everything and we do not seem to be getting anywhere. I think we should call it quits.' Rashid volunteered, opening the conversation.

Vikram was quick to react, 'No Rashid. We are not quitters; let's not throw in the towel. We have fought the battle for too long and put in a lot of effort and money. Think of the team and the other people who have also sweated it out for us. This may seem like the end, but I think it is the darkness before the dawn for us.'

Rashid hesitated at this; he believed in the need to stay the course and Vikram's conviction only strengthened his own. But the events of the past four years were telling him otherwise. 'Let's talk to Shrikant, maybe we need an unbiased view,' he finally opined.

Shrikant Kalburgi was an old friend of Vikram's who was now a successful serial entrepreneur. He had created, scaled and sold at least three independent businesses and was considered an authority on start-ups and entrepreneurship. They had re-established contact with him a few months ago when they had attended a seminar on 'Reality Check for Start-ups', at which Shrikant had been the keynote speaker. He had described some of the challenges and thought processes that tended to limit entrepreneurs from switching strategies, models and people, or dropping ideas and switching to a new business altogether. He had shared how he himself had shut down two of his start-ups; there was no shame in calling it quits, he had stated.

Rashid and Vikram were waiting outside Shrikant's office; his reception was a nice and brightly lit space, with a poster reflecting their thoughts at that moment: 'If you have not failed, you have not tried' it read, very aptly.

They were soon ushered into Shrikant's office by his efficient and cheerful assistant.

Shrikant walked in at precisely 11.30 a.m., their scheduled time for the meeting.

'Hi, Vikram. It's been ages since I last saw you, except for that brief hello at the event sometime back. Hope things are well with you?' enquired Shrikant, shaking hands and giving Vikram a big hug.

He then turned to Rashid, 'You must be his partner, and I believe your entrepreneurial skills are being stretched currently,' he said with a twinkle and a smile.

That helped break the ice and Vikram and Rashid launched into the history of their company and the sequence of events that had led them to where they were today.

'We started this company about four years ago. Ours is a service organization targeting company employee transportation and goods transportation,' began Vikram.

'Rashid is the CEO and I am the COO of the company. We enable companies and suppliers to come together with a strong online-offline model.

'The model is based on owned assets and leased or franchised assets. We own some of the vehicles, but 80 per cent are from enrolled vendors or suppliers.

'We use an online booking platform, which is proprietary, to do the allotment, with a reverse auction engine for the logic.'

'We met with early success, but scaling the same seems to be an insurmountable challenge,' Rashid continued as Vikram paused after explaining their company's model.

'Our team comprises a group of senior professionals, and we have a collective experience of about three hundred years in this space. All our team members have stayed with us till date. The team has sixteen people, so including the two of us, we are a group of eighteen. Four are backroom servicing people, six look after business development and sales, one handles finance, one manages HR and administration, two provide office support and two are runners and courier boys.

'The current challenge is that we continue to burn cash

and we are not acquiring new customers fast enough. The penetration of each account stagnates at 10 per cent.'

'We have invested over US $6 million dollars in the business cumulatively so far. Our revenue and business model has failed and we are unable to modify it to improve the operating parameters,' Vikram admitted.

He continued, 'Our costs are what they were when we started; we have not increased any salaries over four years, nor have we agreed to any increases in technology, rent or other costs.

'Most of our costs are of a fixed nature, and we today burn about 35 lakh rupees a month, all told. The contribution margins of the business are at about 10 per cent on freight, and about 12 per cent on people transportation.

'Rashid and I are now at our wit's end as to what we are unable to see. The pricing is in the upper quartile, the margins are the best in the business, and we have no frills and fancies in the company,' Vikram concluded their brief.

Shrikant heard them out and asked them to send him their financials, business plan, corporate presentation and their client list to help him understand and get into the details of the business. He promised them that he would get back to them the following week.

A week later, Shrikant's assistant called them, requesting their presence at the office at 11.30 a.m. the following morning.

That brought them to today, and they had both dropped everything else to be here. They were now settled in the conference room, awaiting Shrikant's arrival. Both Rashid and Vikram had only one thought on their mind: Would they be given a 'gurumantra' that would pull them out of the mess they found themselves in?

Shrikant walked into the conference room, cheerful and full of life as he normally was.

'Guys, I have done some serious analysis and thinking over the weekend, and I have some rather critical observations and some tough medicine for you. I think the two of you should fortify yourselves with coffee and anything else you may need,' Shrikant started without preamble. 'What I have to say may be unpalatable, but believe me, there are no other options or ways to say this.'

With that, Shrikant began his analysis.

'Your business model is not sustainable in its current format. Though the idea of providing a single source for all transportation needs is novel, it has its inherent challenges.

'The two, goods and people transport, address different teams in the corporates. In the case of goods, your customer is purchase and logistics, while in the case of people, you are dealing with HR and administration in most organizations.

'These are both low margin businesses; a commodity where you are trying to create differentiation. Hence, being asset light is a prerequisite.

'You are positioned neither as a provider of the services, nor the enabler for the two to meet and fructify their business dealings.

'While I appreciate your desire to start with good people, you have created a very heavy fixed cost structure for the business. I am not convinced that you need the profile of people you have.

'Your fixed overheads run to ₹6 crore a year, and in a 10 per cent gross margin business, this means you need ₹60 crore in revenue before you break even in cash terms. Your depreciation is another sword of Damocles you carry.

'To achieve that, you need to have ten times the manpower and have a presence in multiple locations under your current model. Even if you do that today, it will take a few years before any of it starts to pay off.

'Your accumulated losses will be another millstone around your neck. You cannot hope to write them off and turn the corner for another four years.

'I am sorry to say this, but I do not see any way you two can turn this around; the only suggestion I can give is to shut the business down. Start afresh, recast the business model with no baggage, and maybe you will have something that holds promise.

'Get rid of the corporate overheads and the high-cost people; find soldiers and not generals for your team. You can do with one-third the cost of manpower and have a larger team. You cannot do that if you try tooling around with the current structure. You will create bad blood and leave a bitter taste with all.

'There are no shortcuts; announce the shutting down of the business to employees, clients, vendors and partners. Use whatever capital you have to close the company down amicably, without opening yourselves to litigation.

'Go back to the drawing board and start all over again. You may even find that the competition has today made your model redundant, and you may need to explore a strategic change to the model.

'Rebrand and relaunch the business with a new name, people, segmentation and value proposition, or maybe launch a new business altogether. That is for you guys to figure out. If you need my help, please feel free to reach out once you have something on paper, before you launch.

'Sometimes in life, we all need to learn to walk away from a losing proposition and resist the temptation to keep holding onto the past with the excuse that we have spent so much time and effort on it. No point in spending good money behind bad. Cut your losses and walk away.

'As they say, he who runs away lives to fight another day,' ended Shrikant with his usual twinkle.

Rashid and Vikram were stunned. Nothing in their wildest imagination had prepared them for this brutal reality. They had both come hoping they would be given a solution that would pull them out of this morass. Shrikant's suggestion came out of the blue and threw them off track. As they trooped out of Shrikant's office with drooping shoulders and grief writ on their faces, their professional instincts couldn't help but accept the fact that they had just been read the truth sheet. It was something they had been unwilling to confront or think about; but it also dawned on them that it seemed like the most logical and pragmatic thing to do. They looked at each other, nodded in acceptance of the bitter truth and stepped into the sunshine with heavy hearts but a new resolve to move ahead.

Afterword

The set of stories showcased in this book aims to highlight the typical challenges that small and medium enterprises face in India. Each one has a key learning for all those who are, aspire to be, interact with, study, support, coach and contribute in any manner to this eco system.

Here are the takeaways from each story:

- Let Go—Yet Handhold
    - Hiring professionals comes with the responsibility on the entrepreneur to change, handhold and delegate.
- Generate Cash Before Profits
    - In a small business with long working capital cycles, cash flow is a better indicator of success.
- External Investors Must Share The Same Vision
    - Raising capital through external investors should be indulged with care, after ensuring common end

objectives; else get burnt easily.
- Shortcuts Have Long Consequences
    - Complying and adhering to regulations may seem a drag, but shortcuts can have disastrous long-term implications.
- Don't Overdo The Debt
    - Debt is a good augmenter to capital for growth, but overleveraging and large total cost of borrowings are pitfalls to avoid.
- Inorganic Growth Must Have The Right Fit
    - Inorganic growth to scale an organization is easier said than done. Key to success is a strong customer base, cultural fit and shared values.
- Stick To Your Core Values
    - Industry practices and value systems sometimes pose moral dilemmas; do only that which rests well with own set of beliefs and values.
- Segment Well, Position Better
    - Market segmentation, product positioning and pricing play a crucial role in ensuring profitable growth and success for an early stage enterprise.
- Mindshift To Entrepreneurship
    - Making the paradigm change from professionals to budding entrepreneurs calls for managing partners, redefining priorities and recalibrating needs.
- Look Before You Leap
    - Being an entrepreneur often puts us face-to-face with treachery and cunningness; so you need to exercise caution and verify antecedents of all we deal with.
- Legacy Can Be A Liability

- o Acquisitions are almost always difficult to digest and absorb; legacy, questionable value systems, cultural mismatches and dubious business practices are the norm.
- Cut Costs, Not Corners
  - o The need to invest should not be sacrificed at the altar of cost cutting; it can have disastrous ramifications.
- Capital Has Its Colours
  - o The source and quality of capital is as important as the money itself; shortcuts and dubious dealings are an anathema to the long-term survival of the organization.
- Diversify Your Risks
  - o Diversifying risk is the key to success; concentration of business with one supplier, customer or sector is fraught with high probability of failure.
- Manage Investor Expectations
  - o Managing growth and expectations of investors is critical to creating a sustainable business; not doing either can derail the company.
- Feet On The Ground, Head In The Sky
  - o Staying grounded in reality and setting realistic expectations for oneself and partners and stakeholders, is critical to success.
- Knowledge Empowers Decisions
  - o Understanding the market, potential customers and competition is paramount for any new product or service, especially cutting edge and hitherto unknown ones.
- Recast, Recalibrate, Rejuvenate

- Constant assessment of market dynamics, the environmental shifts are critical to recalibrate and recast the business if need be, to stay ahead and be successful.

Acknowledgements

This book is the consequence of a series of discussions and subtle and not-so- subtle goading by my better half, Mala, and would not have transpired but for her incessant efforts. At times critical, at times sceptical, and yet at times inspirational, I cannot but give her the largest share of credit for making this happen.

I cannot miss out my son, whose amazing creativity was a source of inspiration for my attempt at one! Nor can I miss out my mother, whose implicit faith in my ability was a constant source of motivation, to say the least.

It is also a testimony to the encouragement that my dear friends from my school and college days, and professional circles, provided by way of ratification of my intent, with more than a few mugs of cheering. Their incessant questioning for updates only inspired me to finish the task faster.

The numerous clients, partners, well-wishers and acquaintances, who sowed the seeds of the plots, provided the instances, and jogged my memory to recall happenings, all of which feature in the book, as themes and ideas. Their travails, experiences, challenges and reflections are key ingredients in the series of tales which follow.

Most importantly, I would like to acknowledge Harsh Mariwala, Chairman of Marico Industries, who has been a singular role model for the exemplary work he has been doing with small and medium enterprises. I cannot but be humbled by the fact that he consented very readily to write the Foreword for this book, at my behest. I have had the privilege of working with him in my early days, and was always a big fan of his humility, humour and humane approach to the corporate world.

Finally, I would like to acknowledge Arun (K. Vaitheeshwaran), as I fondly call him, for awakening the writer in me, and Dibakar Ghosh and his colleagues at Rupa for painstakingly doing the edits for this first-time writer; it's never easy with beginners, I have heard it said!

Thank you all for making this happen.